Chains of the Heart

ISBN-13: 978-1491298077

ISBN-10: 1491298073

CreateSpace Independent Publishing Platform,

North Charleston, SC

Chains of the Heart

K A Neemeyer

2013

Dedication

There are so many people in my life that I would want to thank for helping me with the inspiration in writing this novel. It would take a couple pages to recognize each and every one. Besides that, there are others, I don't know directly, that I got inspired by the way they talked or interacted with others. Although, I want my family and friends to know that I appreciate the inspiration, if it was a little or a lot.

Of course, a huge thank you has to be said to my husband. He has listened to all my excitement and frustrations while wanting me to do well the entire time. He keeps me centered and focused on my abilities and the important things in life. Thank you.

My sons, Cutter and Cameron, also deserve a big thanks. They have always known how to make me smile when I'm having a bad day. In addition to that, they have made my life both eventful and complete. They are both a huge part of my life that I treasure with all my heart.

Chapter 1

*L*oren gazed at the tree house. Its paint was peeling and the boards were beginning to twist from the years of hot summers and cold winters. But, even with all its flaws, she could still picture it as if it were still new.

It once had fresh green paint with white trim and shutters. On the flat white roof, black lines had been painted to look like shingles. Around the doorway and windows it had pink flowers, drawn by hand, which made it look soft and inviting. Inside it had light pink curtains that would move with the breeze on a warm summer day and the wood used to look fresh and strong.

But now the curtains looked tattered and the wood looked weathered and old. The lines on the roof looked like ugly stains and the pink flowers were barely visible. It didn't look attractive at all.

Loren sighed. She imagined she would have to get out a scraper and some new paint before the weather made it even more unpleasant to look at.

As she gazed at its exterior, she could see her daughter sitting in the doorway with the sun beating down on her back. Her French braid was laying against the back of her sweaty shirt and she held her arms folded across her chest. Her body language suggested she was upset.

Loren felt lost and didn't know how to better the situation. So, for a moment, she admired her daughter's features. She could easily see how they resembled her own.

They both displayed long brown hair and blue eyes with long, dark eyelashes. And, even though Sam was only ten, she was catching up fast to Loren's five foot seven inch height. They both exhibited a trail of freckles on their nose and both of them loved to cuddle. Besides that, they each enjoyed dance. Although Loren was more into ballet while her daughter was into tap and jazz. The only significant difference was their smile.

While Loren found her own smile to be sweet, her daughter's was like her father's. It was breathtaking and people couldn't resist to smile back at her. She made a person want to smile. Loren loved to see her daughter happy and to be able to see it displayed on her face.

Momentarily, she looked past Sam and the tree house to appreciate the view of the rolling hills in her back yard that led to mountains in the far off distance. It was such a beautiful sight to wake to everyday and it made her feel content. Closing her eyes, for just a second, she took in a deep breath and appreciated the fresh air.

Every time she admired the landscape, she knew it was the right decision to buy the twenty acres, in the middle of nowhere, in western

Montana. They were able to see horses grazing in the summer and watch other animals like coyotes, elk, wolves, and so many more. Their two story house sat on top of a hill so they could look for miles at the scenery and wildlife. The winters could get rough but everything else made it worth it.

Since moving there five years earlier, there were no concerns of neighbors having parties in the middle of the night. Plus, no cars speeding in front of their house. It was peace and quiet all the time and Loren didn't have to worry about Sam running in to a busy street.

Of course, there were draw backs too. The distance required them to drive quite a distance to get to the store, to work, to school, or to have Sam visit one of her friend's. And, of course, Loren had to learn to use a gun to ward off any animals that got too close to their home. Although, the animals seemed to keep their distance and stayed far enough away. But, when the stars came out and they laid down on a blanket outside and could stare for miles and miles, she knew it was the perfect place to be.

Loren took another deep breath and then glanced back up at the tree house. She could almost see herself sitting in Sam's place, if she was twenty years younger. But instead, she was standing beneath it trying to figure out the right words to make her daughter feel better.

It had only been three years since Sam's father died in a horrible car accident. It was apparent that she still wasn't ready for anyone to take his place. Which, of course, made the idea of marrying again a very delicate conversation to have with her ten year old daughter. However, she needed Sam to understand it was time for a change.

Shaking her head to herself, Loren understood how she felt. She had undergone the same feelings for the first two years after the accident and his death. Then she met Erik Fisher and everything changed. It wasn't love at first sight, or even close to it. It was a casual "hello" as they walked by each other at the coffee shop, that later turned into a "how are you today?" after a couple months. Then, gradually it became "how about having some coffee together?"

Loren remembered she felt out place and guilty when she and Erik first sat down together. However, after a few more months, she knew Craig, her late husband, would have been okay with her making the choice to move on with her life. No matter how difficult it might be.

But she knew Craig had been the love of her life from the first day they met as teenagers. His hair had been the perfect shade of brown that matched his brown eyes beautifully. He had been a little taller than her, but when she stood on her tiptoes they were eye to eye. However, her favorite feature was his strong jaw line. It would tighten when he was upset, emotional, or when he exercised. She always found everything about him very attractive and couldn't seem to keep her hands off of him. Even when he was sweaty from a work out or tired from a day at work, she needed to have him near her and touch him.

He'd always known how to make her laugh, on the worst days, and how to drive her crazy with his bad habits of leaving coffee grounds in the coffee pot or whiskers in the sink after he shaved. But even after that, he was still the butter to her bread and the frosting to her cake. They were best friends, lovers, and partners in all they did. They had spent every minute they could together and Loren could not wait to kiss his lips after a long day at work. She loved his smile, his laugh, and how he held her tight at night. There was a bond between them some people did not understand and some became jealous of. Then when Samantha, Sam, came into their life, it was the perfect addition to their love.

From the day Sam was born, Craig treated her like a princess and Loren as his queen. And in return, Loren treated him as her king and kept him as happy as she could.

Their love for each other was the kind of love people dreamt of or heard about, but not too many would get the chance to feel in their life time. They had been married ten wonderful years and were together five years before that. Loren could not see them ever being apart.

But then, one sorrowful day, she got the call about the accident. The nurse told her that they did not know how long he would be conscious or alive. His wounds were extreme and he also had internal damage. The nurse told her to get to the hospital as fast as possible.

Loren remembered hanging up the phone and falling to the floor. She thought her heart had been ripped from her chest and stabbed with a knife. She couldn't seem to catch her breath and her body seemed like it was momentarily paralyzed. She knew she couldn't, and shouldn't, drive and had fumbled with the phone to call her sister, Jessie. The next minutes seemed like hours before Jessie ran into the house, kneeled beside her, and gave her a comforting hug.

When they stood up, Loren's legs were weak. Jessie almost had to carry her to the car. By the time they arrived at the hospital it was already too late. Craig had passed away.

Loren had stood next to the hospital bed, smeared with Craig's blood. She held his hand until a nurse finally pulled her away. She couldn't stop the tears from falling or her hands from shaking. She didn't want to leave the hospital, or him.

She could not understand or accept what had happened. Loren felt like she was in a bad dream that she could not wake from. It was like she was in a trance as she went through the motions of making burial plans and picking out clothes for Craig to wear for the last time. However, the worst part was that she found she could not let Sam out of her sight. It terrified her of losing her little girl too.

Although Sam had only been seven years old when Craig died, Loren did not know how to explain or even how to act around her for weeks. She only knew that she had to protect her daughter and keep her safe. She found herself holding Sam's hand everywhere, including the funeral, and wouldn't let go to even receive a hug of condolence. She couldn't.

Now three years later, Sam sat in the tree house, that her dad had built, and Loren stood below it. And as Loren's thoughts were flooded with Craig's image, tears ran down her cheeks and she knew Sam was not ready for such a drastic change. Honestly, she didn't know if she was either. The only thing she knew was that she would have to postpone any idea of a wedding and Erik would have to understand.

Besides that, they had only been dating for a little over a year before Erik asked her to marry him while making dinner. He didn't have a ring or get down on one knee. He didn't quote a poem or take her on a hot air balloon ride. He simply asked the question casually and when Loren said she would think about it, he had promised a beautiful ring to go on her finger.

Since then Loren had been thinking for three weeks how to tell Sam. She knew she would have issues with the decision and Loren needed her approval. She didn't want to marry Erik and have Sam resent her or him in the future.

Loren shook her head and tried to concentrate on Sam. She wiped her eyes before she shielded them from the setting sun with her hand. She watched as her daughter turned so her back was to her. "Sam, please come down. It's so hot out today and the air conditioner would feel really good right now. I understand how you feel and I won't do anything." She paused a moment to lick her dry lips and stared at Sam for any kind of a reaction. Sam remained motionless and Loren began to feel like she was talking to the tree instead of her daughter. "I'm not saying that it will never happen in the future, but . . . for right now, it won't. Sweetie, he hasn't even given me an engagement ring. Now, let's go get a bowl of ice cream and cool down. I'm sure you have to go to the bathroom too after drinking all that lemonade earlier."

Loren watched as Sam shrugged her shoulders and lowered her head. She turned to come down the ladder and Loren knew she had won the battle. At least for now.

Sam jumped to the ground and looked at her mom. She spoke with bitterness and hurt. "The only reason I'm coming down is because *I* want to and because ice cream sounds good," she said. Then she put her head back down so Loren couldn't see her eyes.

Loren threw her arms around her daughter's sweaty shoulders and gave her a soft squeeze. "Baby, I know things are changing, but I need you beside me, not fighting me. We're a team, you and I, and I hope we always will be. I love you Sammie bear." Loren grabbed Sam's hand and tugged to get her to walk towards the house.

Sam was reluctant to walk with her but then gave a quick smile, tagged Loren on the arm, and ran to the house yelling, "Tag, you're it."

Loren chased after her and they laughed as they went inside. Just as Loren grabbed the ice cream, she saw a car coming up the driveway. She quickly scooped ice cream into the bowls and glanced at the window to see it was Erik. "Sammie bear, why don't you take your ice cream to your room so I can talk to Erik."

Loren watched Sam hop up the stairs and suddenly felt nervous when she saw Erik walk up the sidewalk towards the house. Taking a bite of ice cream, she tried to push the feeling away and concentrated on the man walking towards her. The first thing she noticed was his dark blonde hair with curls that was just long enough for her to run her fingers through. Then she admired his six foot frame with nice muscles from going to the gym at least three times a week. She smirked and thought he looked good as he walked towards her wearing jean shorts and a t-shirt. And as she stared into his big brown eyes, it made her nervous all over again.

He stepped inside, gave her a quick kiss on the cheek, and frowned. Erik said, "I know that look. What's wrong?"

Loren twisted her hands and looked at the wood floor. This wasn't a conversation she was looking forward to. "Well, I have some bad news. I tried to talk to Sam about us getting married and it didn't go so good."

Erik took Loren's hand into his before he smiled. "Honestly, I wasn't expecting a good response from her. I kind of imagined that she'd not like the idea."

Loren couldn't believe his reaction. "Really? I mean, I thought you'd be upset. I'm sorry but I don't think I can go against her right now."

Erik walked into the kitchen and momentarily admired the ledge stone around the oven and wood floors throughout the room before he sat down and let out a loud sigh. "I know you can't. That's what I love about you. You're such a good mom and you go with what your heart tells you. I have to say that I'm a little hurt, but I'm not going to get mad and storm away. I already knew the circumstances and want *both* of you to be happy. I'm not going anywhere and we can give Sam as much time as she needs. Three years isn't a lot of time to a kid sometimes."

Loren sat in a chair next to Erik and stared at him. She had been so nervous to talk to Sam and now he was fine with how she reacted? How was he fine with it? He'd been the one to ask her a few weeks ago and seemed so eager to be husband and wife. And who promised to give her the best engagement ring after he received Sam's blessing. Now he sat calmly and said he was okay with it? "I don't know what to say. I guess I thought that you would be a little more . . . I don't know."

Erik grinned. "I tell you what. I was really looking forward to you saying yes and Sam jumping into my arms happy with the decision to become a family. I really was. But I know that Sam is Craig's little girl and I don't want to force anything on her. If that means that you and I are engaged for another year, or five years, that's how it is. I know you don't have a ring yet, but I still consider us engaged and I hope you do too." He gave her a soft hug and then he gently rubbed her back. He spoke softly. "I love Sam and want her as happy as I want to make you. I know I could never replace Craig. From the stories I have heard from the both of you, and others in the town, the love you two had was pretty special."

Loren had tears stream down her face and she didn't even try to wipe them away. She looked into Erik's brown eyes and could see the hurt in them. She reached for his hand. "Erik, I'm so happy to have you in my life. After Craig's death I never thought I would feel love for another man until you came along. We've been together for a little over a year and you've opened my heart again. And you being so understanding right now, shows me what a truly wonderful man you are. Thank you."

"Hey, I have two ladies to keep happy and I know one won't be if the other isn't." Erik looked up the stairs towards Sam's room. "Is she in her room? I think I should talk to her."

Loren nodded her head and watched Erik stand up, go up the steps, and knock gently on Sam's door before he opened it and went inside. He didn't close the door, but he spoke softly and Loren couldn't understand what he was saying. She couldn't hear Sam say anything and wondered if she should go in to make sure everything was alright. Just as she stood up, Erik came out, closing the door gently behind him. He walked back to the kitchen and sat down and grabbed Loren's hands. He sighed and smiled.

Loren couldn't stand not knowing what he said or why he was smiling. "Well? What did she say? What did you say?"

Erik kept smiling and shook his head. "When I opened the door I saw her sitting next to the window, reading a book. I told her that I understand and that I won't push the issue anymore. She shrugged her shoulders. That was it."

Loren bit her lip. "Would you like me to talk to her? I think she should have given you more of a response then what she did."

She went to the refrigerator to look for something to drink. She grabbed a bottle of water for herself and Erik and reached for a couple of glasses. Just as she set the glasses on the table, she heard Sam's bedroom door open.

Sam came into the kitchen and sat in Loren's chair. She gazed at the flower arrangement on the table while touching the leaves. "Hey Erik? Well, I just wanted to tell you that I . . . well, that I liked that you talked to me. I really do like you, and stuff, but I just don't think I could ever have someone else in my mom's room. My dad should be the only one that was ever there. Do you get what I'm saying?" Sam sighed. She kept staring at the flowers.

Erik glanced at Loren and then touched Sam's hand. "Thank you for coming out to talk to me. I'm sure that was difficult." He patted Sam's hand and then folded them in front of him on the table. "I just wanted to let you know that I want both of you happy. I love your mom very much and I love you too. I think you're both the best women that I've ever met. I really do want to marry your mom and be a family, but I won't right now. Are we still okay, you and I?"

Sam stood up, nodded her head to agree, and headed back to her bedroom. She closed her door quietly before they heard music coming from behind it.

Loren sat down and poured her and Erik some water. She took a deep breath and was proud of her daughter. She smiled to herself and couldn't believe what a wonderful young woman Sam was becoming. Craig would be so proud of her and Loren wished he could be next to her right now.

With that thought, Loren's heart seemed to break. She missed Craig and having Erik beside her didn't help her feel better at the moment. She wondered if she would ever be able to move on without Craig or if she was going to have to force herself. What if she was thinking of marrying Erik just to try and move on? What if Sam was seeing more than she was?

Erik seemed to sense her discomfort. "Are you alright? Did I say something wrong?"

"No, no, you didn't. You said the perfect words and I'm so proud of Sam and so happy to have you in my life. It's just . . ."

"It's just Craig? Right?"

"Yeah, I'm sorry."

"Loren, don't ever tell me that you're sorry for thinking of someone that you loved. It's pretty clear that marriage between you and I shouldn't even be on the table right now." Erik took a drink of the water and stood up next to the table. He held out his hands for Loren to stand up and gave her a hug. "Just know that I'm here when you're ready. I need to get going to a job site before they quit for the day, so I'll talk to you later."

Loren didn't know what to say. She looked at his hands and squeezed them.

Erik headed to the door. "Anyways, I'll give you a call tonight. Love you Loren."

"I love you too. I'll talk to you later then." Loren gave Erik a kiss and closed the door.

She started to head towards Sam's bedroom, but instead turned towards her own. When she opened the door she almost expected Craig to be laying on the bed taking a nap or reading one of his favorite books. Her heart ached for him and she needed him to tell her if he was alright with her decisions.

Loren grabbed her favorite necklace from her dresser and wrapped the chain around her fingers and fell back onto the bed. Holding the necklace up, she watched as the diamonds, within a gold heart, sparkled with the sun cascading through the window. She was mesmerized by the shiny gold and diamonds and remembered the day Craig had given it to her.

It hadn't been for a birthday or anniversary or any other occasion. It was a few months into their marriage and Loren was folding laundry in the living room. He came home, asked her to close her eyes, and put the necklace in her hands. She was shocked when she first saw it.

"What's this for?" she had asked astounded by its beauty.

Craig had looked at her with such love she thought she was going to burst. He said, "I saw this in the store window and I just knew that I wanted to give it to you. I couldn't wait for a special time of the year. I just wanted you to know that you mean so much to me and that your heart has so much to give. You have the biggest, kindest, loving heart I've ever known. I wanted to give you this so that you never forget what you have. I believe the heart is the most important thing. If you don't have heart, then you don't have anything. I do mean this in an emotional meaning, not physical one."

Loren admired the necklace and it seemed like Craig was right beside her as she held it in her hands. She was lost in her thoughts and didn't hear Sam walk into her room.

"Mom? Are you okay? Why are you crying?"

Loren sat up and hadn't even noticed the tears flowing down her cheeks. She wiped them away and gave Sam a hug. "I'm fine Sammie bear. I was just remembering the day your dad gave me this. I guess I got caught up in the memory."

"Is this about Erik? I do like him. It's just . . ."

"You don't have to explain yourself. I feel the same way. Your dad is still part of our lives and always will be. I don't know if I'll ever be able to marry Erik. I still love your dad too much."

"No. You need to marry him."

Loren looked at Sam confused. "Now you want me to marry him?"

Sam jumped up on the bed and laid her head on Loren's lap. "I want us to be a family. I'm just scared that if we do that I'll forget daddy. I don't want to ever forget him. I feel like the memories I have are already starting to go away. I have to look at his picture to remember him. I don't see him in my mind like I use too. That scares me." She started to cry.

Loren held Sam in her arms. "Sweetie, neither one of us will ever forget him. He was a wonderful man and daddy and meant the world to me and you. I'll tell you stories about him any time you want. I have a lot of them. We can watch videos with him in it or go through pictures." Loren took a deep breath.

"I'll always remember how he held you close as a baby and played tea party with you when you were little. I will always remember when he built your tree house and had blisters on his fingers from hitting them with the hammer. I'll never forget his smile, because you have the same one. I see him every time you smile. Did you know that?"

Sam wiped her eyes and looked up at Loren shyly. "Really? You think of him when I smile?"

"Yep. Every time."

Sam smiled a huge smile and hugged her mom. "Did you see him?"

Loren hugged Sam again. "Yes I did, Sammie bear. Yes I did."

Chapter 2

Loren dropped Sam off at a neighbor's and headed to meet her sister, Jessie. She needed to forget about losing Craig and marrying Erik. She needed to forget her job and every other stress she was feeling. She needed a night out.

As she parked in front of the house, she saw the curtains move and saw a glimpse of Jessie's fiancé behind them. Loren didn't know if he liked her taking Jessie to a bar, but she didn't care. Not tonight.

As Jessie stepped out of the house, Loren still couldn't get over how beautiful her older sister looked. Tonight she was wearing a pair of skinny jeans with black boots and a snug black tank top. Loren thought she looked picturesque, although Jessie would never think that. Jessie had never thought she was pretty and Loren thought that made her even more beautiful.

She had long brown hair that showed the perfect amount of wave to it along with brown eyes that seemed to turn black when she was extremely happy or sad. She was almost six foot tall and a petite figure. Her facial features looked like a model from a magazine and her smile was hypnotizing. She didn't resemble anyone in their family and even Jessie questioned their parent's if she was adopted. But their parent's had told her that she resembled an aunt from years ago and left it at that.

Jessie walked to the Jeep and waved to her fiancé, who was now looking out of the door. She sat down in the passenger seat and slammed the door. She let out a breath. "I think I need this night as much as you. Derik has been driving me crazy lately. He keeps pushing the issue of having kids after we're married and I don't know if I want them or not. What am I supposed to do about that? I'm not having children if I don't feel I would be a good mom."

Loren started her Jeep and pulled away from the curb. "Not a good mom? Are you nuts? You were basically my mom while we were growing up. I think you did a pretty good job."

"You know what I mean. Mom and dad were on business trips a lot for work, but I had them to fall back on when they were home. But, if I have kids of my own, they would be mine to take care of until I was old and gray."

Loren sighed. "Well, I think you would be an awesome mom and I think Sam would love a little cousin. But it's not my decision. I'll help you how I can, but I don't want you doing something you'll regret in a few years. You can't return them."

"I know, right. Why can't he understand that? He doesn't have to get the stretch marks and puke for six months. Or for that matter, he doesn't have something come out of him that should be physically impossible to come out of a human."

"Okay Jess, can we stop with the guy and kid talk? I wanted to escape all of that for one night."

Jessie looked at Loren and smiled. "Escape guys? The way you look? Good luck."

Loren rolled her eyes and they didn't talk again until they parked at the "Tilted Glass Bar and Grill". They went into the dimly lit bar and found a booth not too far from the bathrooms. Jessie ordered them each a beer and excused herself to check her make-up.

Loren looked around, while she waited for her drink, and noticed a bunch of college age guys playing a game of darts and a group of older men playing a game of pool. She saw them glance her way, but she didn't think anything of it. She wasn't there to find a new friend or hook up with anyone for the night.

Looking towards the bar area to see if the waitress was getting her a drink, she could see there were a few women, but they looked like they were part of a bachelorette party and were self-involved with getting the future bride to drink as many shots of liquor as they could. Loren smiled to herself when she thought back to her bachelorette party, but then quickly pushed the thought away. She was determined to get away from the memories for just one night.

Taking a deep breath, she sat back in her seat and a man, who looked to be in his early thirties, seated himself across from her and stared. He rested his cheek on his hand and looked at her lovingly.

He said, "Did you fall from heaven? You look like you did. I think we were meant to be together tonight."

Loren tried not to laugh. She studied his face and noticed he had brown hair and blue eyes and didn't look like he tried to shave in days. When she looked at his hands she could see the indentation where a wedding ring would have been. She knew he was either still married and looking for a one night stand or recently separated and looking for the same thing. Either way she wasn't interested. "Yeah, I don't think that's gonna happen. I came in here to have a few drinks. That's all. So . . . I think you should go."

"You're gonna be like that huh? Well, I think you need a good man in your life and you're looking at him. I work for a respectable accounting firm and have a hefty bank account. I'm sure you wouldn't mind that, would you?"

"Hmm . . . let me think about it?" Loren put her finger on her chin and tapped it three times. "Well, I thought about it and I'm going to pass. Thanks for the wonderful offer, but no thanks."

"You're going to pass . . ."

Jessie interrupted, "The girl said to take a hike. Take the hint dude!"

The man whipped his head around, looked at Jessie with lust in his eyes, and stood up. "Wow! It's my lucky night. I have two angels to talk to."

Jessie put her finger in the man's face. "Now listen here, we're not interested. Do you get it? Now take a flying leap."

The man stared at Jessie for a few seconds before he heaved a sigh and walked away. He rejoined some men sitting at a corner table and shook his head in defeat.

Jessie sat down and flipped her long brown hair to one side. "Seriously? I leave for two minutes and you have them rolling on you already?"

"Yeah, I guess. We haven't even gotten a beer yet." Loren said as she looked around for the waitress.

"She is coming right now. Maybe we need to order another one right away. I think they're going to taste good tonight."

Loren smiled and took a long drink of her beer the moment the waitress sat it on the table. She liked the coolness on her throat and the taste on her tongue. She took another drink and set it down to grab a bowl of pretzels to snack on. "So, what do you want to talk about that isn't man related?"

"Well, how about the coffee shop? How's that going?"

"Work? I guess it is going okay. "Good Mornings" pretty much runs itself after being open for the last four years. I've found the best employees and they seem to treat me and the customers good. I probably pay them a little too much, but I want to keep them. I have a lot more spare time for myself and I want to keep it that way. Especially with it being summer time and I want to spend as much time with Sammie bear as I can. She is growing up way too fast." Loren took a drink of her beer and sat back in her seat. "I just wish I could figure out the rest of my life."

"Join the club. Between working at the flower shop and trying to figure out the wedding stuff, I'm pretty well spent by the end of the day. I don't know if owning my own business was the right choice. I mean I like it a lot, but it gets stressful sometimes. I seriously live for the weekends anymore. And I have to say that tonight was the perfect time to get out."

Loren admired her sister, as she spoke, and noticed she wasn't wearing her engagement ring. "Hey Jess, where's your ring?"

Jess put her right hand over her left to hide her fingers. "I don't know. I guess I forgot to put it on after my shower."

"What's going on? Are you and Derik having troubles more than the kid thing?"

"Hell Loren! We're not supposed to talk about that stuff. Let's just enjoy the night, okay?"

Loren didn't know what to think. She thought that Jessie and Derik made a perfect couple. If they couldn't make it, then who could. Why should she even try with Erik if they couldn't make it?

Loren's thoughts were interrupted when two men came to their table.

A man with brown hair and green eyes spoke first. "Hey ladies. We noticed that you were alone and we're alone so we thought . . ."

Loren was irritated and interrupted him. "What is it with you men? Why can't two women sit and have a drink without getting harassed? Why do we have to hide out in our homes having little parties so we don't have to get approached every time we're in a bar? Why can't you all just leave us alone?"

The second man, with red hair and green eyes, glared at Loren. He curled his lips and looked at her with contempt. He pointed his finger at her and spoke with hate in his voice. "You know, its women like you that make us guys uncomfortable. Do you think that you're better than us to talk like that? I thought you were pretty when we walked over here but now I think you are the ugliest woman I have ever seen. You're a dog!" He screamed into Loren's face. "And for your information, this is a bar! This a place for men and women to hook up. If you don't like it then leave. Go stay in your little house and bake cookies."

Loren smiled at the man and waited for him to stop yelling. She spoke soft and casual. "Oh, did you get your feelings hurt? Sorry if I didn't make your night my majesty."

The man shook his head side to side and his face started to turn red. "You little . . . you really think that you are something huh?"

Loren didn't react to the man's harshness. She sat idle and acted bored. "No sir, I don't. I'm just an average girl who's out for the night. I'm not looking for a guy or a one night stand. I'm not here to make flirtatious eyes at people to get attention. I'm not here to strut around and shake my tail feather. I'm not here to find the catch of the day. No, I'm only here to have a drink and talk to my sister. I really do hope that's alright with you."

The red haired man stepped towards Loren and the other man put his arm around him to hold him back. He apologized for the man's behavior and turned to leave, making the red haired man go with him.

Loren sat baffled and didn't know what had just happened. She didn't know how it started or how she kept her cool through it all. She took a long drink of her beer and stared at her sister over the bottle. She took a second drink and grabbed Jessie's hand. "What the hell was that? Why didn't you stop me?"

Jessie smiled. "Honestly, I was impressed and wanted to see how far you'd take it. I would've had your back. I didn't think you had it in you Loren. You have more spit fire in you then I give you credit for." Jessie looked around at the people in the bar. "I think you needed to let off a little steam and that little twerp was just the ticket. The only difference between me and you is I would have hit the jerk."

She looked back at Loren. "Anyways, I didn't come in here to get man handled either. I get enough of that at home. I'm glad you said it to him or I would have."

"What does that mean? Man handled at home?" Loren asked.

"Don't worry about it. He has just been really pushy lately. I'm starting to think he wants to get me pregnant so he has a hold on me the rest of our lives. But enough of that. We weren't going to talk about that stuff tonight."

Loren sat silent for a moment. She was stunned by her own actions, moments ago, and now with what her sister was telling her. She knew she really wasn't in the mood to get into a big discussion about men tonight, so she decided to forget about both of their man issues. "Alright, but you know you can talk to me anytime." She looked around the bar and saw the red haired man glare at her from across the room. Looking away, the thought of Erik crossed her mind. "I don't want to talk about guys anymore, but I do want to ask one question since we're on the man conversation. Should I marry Erik or should I stay single the rest of my life?"

Jessie looked at Loren with a surprised expression. "What do you mean? I thought he already asked you?"

"You know what? Just forget it. We're not supposed to talk about that stuff tonight."

"No way. You're not getting out of this one. Erik is the perfect guy for you. He has been understanding and has put up with your emotional roller coaster for over a year. What else could you ask for?"

Loren sighed. She knew she shouldn't have brought Erik into the conversation. "I know, it's just that Sam isn't ready and I don't know if I am either. I just don't know if it's the right choice. I mean it has only been three years since Craig passed. What's the waiting period on remarrying? Is there a waiting period? There's no manual as far as I know." Loren pushed her hair behind her ears. "I'm just confused. I need Craig to tell me it is alright."

Jessie rolled her eyes. "For heaven's sake Loren. Craig loved you so much and he would want you to happy without him. I'm sure he would have wanted you to be married again already. He loved you that much." Jessie paused and pulled the label off of her bottle of beer. She folded it several times until she could fold it no more. She looked up at Loren and tilted her head. "Erik makes you happy doesn't he? I know he does. I've seen how you smile around him and how he looks at you when you aren't looking. He's in love with you and tries to show it all the time. I bet you told him the marriage would have to wait and he was okay with it, right?"

Loren nodded her head.

"See. He would do anything to have you in his life. He's the perfect man for you without Craig around. I mean Craig was the ultimate perfect man, but Erik comes in at a close second. Not too many people would get two awesome guys in one life time. Come on Loren, wake up and smell the coffee."

Loren knew that Jessie was right. She needed it said out loud. She swallowed the last of her beer and the waitress brought another one, just as fast. They sat without talking and Loren was comfortable with the silence.

Chapter 3

*E*rik and Loren headed to the local museum. With the beautiful morning coolness, they walked around the outside exhibits. They wanted to see as much as they could before the afternoon heat took hold and chased them indoors.

Loren first admired the old farming machinery. As she walked, she wondered if she should bring up the adventure she had with her sister at the bar but decided against it. She didn't want Erik to get upset with another man being rude to her. So instead she kept her thoughts to herself and appreciated all the hard work it took to live in the old times. Looking at Erik, she grinned and felt the muscles on his arm. "Could you see yourself using this stuff to supply for your family? I think you'd have the muscle for it." She paused. "That lifestyle must have been hard. Although, I think we've gotten really spoiled with all the new technology."

Erik stared at a hand plow and grinned. "Yeah, I don't think I'd live very long in those days. I like heading to a grocery store instead of growing, picking, grinding, and making my own bread. But I do have to say that it's all very impressive. I don't consider myself to be a weak man, but those people were tougher than me."

Loren giggled. "Yeah, I can't see myself doing the hard work all the time either."

They continued walking and enjoyed each other's company. After a few minutes Erik stopped in his tracks and turned towards Loren. "Did I tell you what happened yesterday?"

Loren looked at him inquisitively. "No. what happened?"

"Well, when I was on my way home, I decided to take a short cut on some back roads. When I came to a stop sign about a mile from my place, I saw some little ears sticking out from the tall grass in the ditch. It got me curious. I didn't know if it was a fawn or what."

"What was it?" Loren asked.

"It was a dog."

"A dog? A stray or did it have a collar?"

"Nope. No collar, no tags. Kind of a cute little thing. I'd say about mid-size with black, gray, and brown markings on white fur. She's a sweetie too."

"You went and touched it? You could have been bitten," Loren said.

"Well, I wasn't. She's as sweet as they come and had a very good demeanor and everything. She even knew a few commands like sit and lay down."

"So what did you do? Take her to the dog shelter?"

"No . . . I took her home."

Loren put her hands on her hips. "You did what?"

"Hey, I couldn't leave her there. She looked hungry and needed a bath."

"That's kind of big news. Why didn't you tell me on the way here?"

Erik scratched his head. "I don't know. I guess I'm not use to her yet and I was mesmerized by you."

Loren smiled and it faded just as quickly. "You going to keep her? I mean . . . you're not going to keep her, are you?"

Erik looked confused. "Why wouldn't I? She's a good dog and I'm tired of being in my house by myself all the time." He nudged Loren on the shoulder. "Hint, hint," he said and winked.

Loren didn't know what to think. Was this a tactic to get her to marry him faster? Did she have to take the dog into her home also when they did get married? Although, she knew Sam would love to have a dog around the house.

She continued to walk and look at the old artifacts even though her mind wasn't actually seeing them. She glanced over at Erik and he was smiling at her. "What?"

"I knew you'd freak out about it. You're trying hard to keep it hidden, but I know you."
"It's fine. It's just . . ."

Erik interrupted. "Just wait til you meet her. Your heart will melt just like mine."

Loren tried to smile. She was still having a hard time with letting Erik into her heart and home. Now he wants a dog in the mix too? Loren slowed her pace and then stopped. She turned towards Erik and had a confused look on her face. "Okay. If we get married . . ."

"If we get married?" Erik asked.

"Fine. *When* we get married you're still going to come live with me right?"

"Was planning on it. Why? You have a problem with a dog Loren?"

"I guess I'll find out. We didn't have too many pets when we were kids. I'm sure it'll be alright," Loren said. She tried to forget about the dog. But the idea of him having a pet kept creeping back into her mind.

There was obviously a lot she didn't know about Erik. She never knew that he was an animal person. Nor did she think he would pick an animal up from the side of the road. She began to wonder what else she didn't know about him. They had been dating for quite some time. Maybe she didn't ask enough questions.

Trying to think of something new to ask, Loren thought of her own past. "Alright, you have two brothers and one sister. I've met one brother and your sister, but I've never met your other brother or parent's. Why?"

Erik puckered his lips and tried to think. "Well, the other brother and I can't stand to be around each other. Never have. We would fight from the moment we got up until the moment we went to sleep. I don't even know what started it all. And my parent's, well, that's another story. For one, they live in Florida and that's quite a distance to stop by and say hello. I haven't seen them for a couple years. Although, my mom's asked to talk to you a couple times." Erik held Loren's hand and kissed it. "I'm sure you'll meet them if we ever get a wedding date set."

Loren got mad. "Come on. I had just told you that I need time. I thought you respected that."

Erik giggled. "Gees Loren. Calm down. It was a joke."

"Not a very good joke," Loren responded.

"Fine. Fine. Any other questions? I kind of like you asking me about stuff. You don't do it very much."

"Well . . . have you had any other pets growing up?"

Erik grinned. "Oh yeah. I had everything from frogs and snakes to goats. I loved and still love animals. I would get a new pet all the time. If they came from my parent's or me finding them on my own. I had my bedroom and our garage filled with aquariums and homemade cages." He paused and kicked the dirt on the ground. "Come to think of it, I think that's why my brother and I fought all the time. We shared a room when we were kids. I guess he wasn't the animal lover that I am."

Loren snickered. "I suppose that could be it. What other hobbies did you have?"

Erik put his hands in his back pockets and laughed. He thought about it for a few seconds and started to laugh again. "I had all kinds of hobbies. I would take stuff apart and try to put it back together. Which could be another reason my brother has a problem with me. I remember taking his radio apart and not quite getting it to work again. Anyways, I fidgeted in the garage a lot. I designed the cages for my pets and got pretty extravagant with some of them. The hamsters had a log cabin to live in and the cats loved the scratching posts I made. I built bird houses, dog houses and anything else I could think of. Guess that's how I became an architect."

Loren was amazed. She didn't know any of this. Why didn't she know any of this? Why hadn't she asked in the past? She shook her head.

Erik looked at her confused. "What's wrong?"

"I'm mad."

"You're mad? About what?"

"I'm mad because I didn't know any of this about you. I should know all of this. I should know you better than what I do. I'm kind of embarrassed."

Erik gave her a hug. "Don't be. I'm sure there's a lot I don't know about you either. We haven't been together that long. I mean, we don't spend twenty four hours a day talking. Of course there's going to be stuff we don't know. That's actually kind of good isn't it? That way we always have something to talk about later. And something new to discover."

Loren relaxed. She knew he was right. Although she still felt she should know more about him, she was okay with it for now.

She could feel the sun begin to make her shirt stick to her back from the heat. She glanced at Erik and saw he had sweat on his forehead too. "Want to head inside and see if there is something for us to drink somewhere? I'm getting pretty thirsty and hot out here."

Erik nodded his head and turned towards a big building with bear hides tacked to the doors. When they stepped inside and let their eyes adjust to the light, Loren was amazed. There was so much to see and explore. She definitely knew she would have to bring Sam here to explore with her.

They found a little café within the building and sat down at a small wooden table. Loren drank her tea from a straw and looked around. "Did you go to museums as a kid? We never did. I think I went to one on a fieldtrip for school."

"You've lived a sheltered life. Not going to museums, shameful," he teased.

Loren nodded her head at him and took another sip of her tea. "I guess I did. But it doesn't sound like I had cool parents like you. Mine would never let us have a pet just because we found it.

They would lecture us on rabies and infections until we would be too scared to want one. However we did have a little dog when we were teenagers. That took years of begging to get her. She died before I graduated. She must have been pretty old before we even got her. I don't really remember."

"That's horrible. No wonder you freaked out about me getting a dog. And off the road nonetheless."

"Well actually, before Craig's accident, he was trying to talk me into getting a cat or dog. He had heard that kids get less allergies if they are around the pet dander and would build a tolerance to it. We had actually agreed to go to the shelter and look the week he died."

Erik frowned. "I'm sorry about that. See, that's something I didn't know either."

Loren leaned back in her seat and thought back to that week. She remembered trying to get herself ready to have a pet. She had already envisioned where to have the food and litter box for a cat. Then she had looked online for pet toys and how to pick a dog that was right for them. But then Craig had the accident and she couldn't do it without him. She didn't want to do it without him.

Loren pushed the thought away and concentrated on Erik. She needed to learn to do a better job at that. She needed to quit letting her past interfere with her present and future.

Watching him drink his soda, Loren admired his features and curls in his hair. His hair seemed to get curlier with the humidity and when he began to sweat. She thought it was cute. She almost reached to run her fingers through it, but then decided against it. It wasn't the place or time.

After they were done with their drinks, they began to explore the large building. Loren felt like a little kid as she ran from display to display. She would grab Erik's hand and drag him along so he could enjoy it with her.

Erik laughed. "I wish I would have known you as a kid. I think we would have had fun together. You could have been my sidekick and fellow explorer. We could've explored the lake by my house. I could have taught you how to catch a turtle off the bottom of the lake or catch a frog in mid jump. We would've had fun."

Loren grinned. "We're not old. We can still have fun can't we? I know a couple lakes we could go to. I'm up for the challenge if you are."

Erik pulled her close to him and breathed the smell of her hair. "I love you Loren. I truly think that we're going to have a wonderful life together if it involves wedding vows or not. I think we're going to have a lot of adventures to experience together too. I can't wait to have so many memories with you to tell when we're old and gray."

    She hugged him tight and kissed him softly on the lips. "I love you too. But I think we should get moving so we can create a new memory right now."

Chapter 4

Sam played her Barbie's while Loren weeded her garden. It was a beautiful Saturday with big fluffy clouds floating by and a soft breeze to fight off the heat from the sun. The temperature wasn't stifling hot, but warm enough to make sweat droplets form on the back of Loren's neck. She wiped it away with her garden glove and knew she had left a trail of dirt in its place, but didn't care. They weren't planning on anyone coming over and she wasn't going to leave either. It was going to be a relaxing day of working in the garden followed by a swim in the pool.

Finishing up with the last row of radishes, Loren stood up and stretched her back. She shielded her eyes and looked up towards the sun and decided it was time for a break. She glanced back at the house and watched as Sam sat in a lounge chair and rummaged through a box of Barbie clothes to find the perfect outfit. Grinning, she gathered her gardening tools and threw them into a wagon. It was the same wagon that Sam had as a baby and Loren had later converted it into her own personal gardening carriage.

She sprayed her hands off with a hose along with her feet and legs. Walking back to the house, Loren wiped her forehead with the back of her hand and sat next to Sam. "Ready for a swim? I know I am."

"I've been ready for the last hour."

Loren smiled at her daughter. "Well then, maybe you should've come over to help me instead of playing with your Barbie dolls."

"But mom, I had to get them ready to go in the pool too. I put their swimsuits on. See." She showed Loren two of her dolls that were dressed in glittery swimsuits and water shoes.

Just as they headed into the house to change into their swimsuits, a car came up the driveway.

Sam stomped her foot on the ground and folded her arms in front of her. "Ah man. I wanted to swim. Who is it mom?"

Loren strained to see the vehicle through the dust flying around it from the gravel road. Finally, when it was almost to the house, she recognized the blue SUV. "It's your Aunt Jessie. Wonder what she's doing here. I thought she'd be at work all day."

Sam grinned and started to run towards the slowing car. When Jessie opened the door Sam took a step back and her smile faded. "What happened Aunt Jessie? You look horrible."

"Thanks Sammie. That's what a girl likes to hear. Where's your mom?"

Loren stood in the shade under the eve of the house. "I'm right here. What's going on sis?"

Jessie played with Sam's hair and walked up to the house. "Let's just say that the wedding's off."

Sam grabbed Jessie's arm and twirled under it. "The weddings off? Why?"

Jessie looked at Loren and frowned. "I guess I don't want to be a mom and that was a deal breaker."

Loren's heart hurt for her sister. Jessie and Derik had dated for three years and were planning their wedding for almost an entire year. They planned a garden wedding with their vows being said under a gazebo with flowers everywhere. There colors were pink and green and Loren had already purchased her dress. It was supposed to take place in two months. "A deal breaker huh? I guess it is better the invites haven't been sent out yet. I'm so sorry Jess. When did this all go down?"

"It went on until I drove here and started about twelve hours ago. He was relentless. Every time I would fall asleep he would cuddle up to me and try to . . . let's say . . ." She glanced at Sam. "Let's say he tried to talk me into seeing things his way. He wouldn't let me sleep, go to work, or even pee without him watching. So I waited until he finally dozed off and headed here." Jessie glanced at Sam. "Hey pip squeak. Why don't you go into the house for a second? Would you please?"

Sam let her arms drop to her sides and pouted. "Man, I miss all the good stuff. Are we still gonna swim?" she asked and looked at Loren for an answer.

"Go get your swimsuit on and we'll meet you in the back yard. Maybe Aunt Jess would want to swim too?" Loren asked and looked to her sister for a response.

"No pool time for me. If it's alright I would like to go crash for a while in your bed. I don't think I got an hour of sleep. I ended up playing the music loud and had the windows down just so I wouldn't fall asleep on the way here."

Loren suddenly felt panicky.

Jessie shook her head. "I'm sorry Loren. I was fine driving. I really was. I'm sorry for saying anything."

Loren looked at Jessie and frowned. "You're fine. It's just *you know* they never figured out if Craig fell asleep or swerved to miss something. Just call me if you ever need a ride, okay?"

"Yes I will. And I'm sorry. Now can I go to bed? I'm going to fall asleep standing up pretty quick."

Loren followed her sister into the house and grabbed her swimsuit and a couple towels from the bathroom connected to her bedroom. Before she left the room, Jessie was already asleep on the bed. Loren covered her with a blanket and closed the door quietly before she joined Sam in the backyard for a dip in the pool.

A few hours later the three of them sat on the patio and watched as the sun set and left a countless number of stars behind. It was a beautiful summer night with a soft breeze and no clouds to hide the beautiful display of the sky. Sam pulled a blanket around her shoulders and stared at the heavens. She tried to find the constellations she learned in school while Loren and Jessie sipped on a glass of wine. Loren laid in a lounge chair and was hypnotized by the flames moving within the outdoor fireplace.

"Hello?"

Loren looked towards Jessie and smiled. "Sorry, were you talking to me?"

"Ah, yeah I was. Where were you?"

"Lost in the beauty of the flames. It's so peaceful."

"Okay, well anyways, I was trying to tell you about Derik while Sam is caught up with the stars."

Loren sat up in her chair. "I'm giving you my full attention."

Jessie took a sip of her wine and looked up at the night sky. "Why can't I find a guy like you? I mean, you had Craig and now Erik. I'm jealous of you, but happy at the same time. I just wish that Derik was a little like them. Since we started dating he has become controlling and now the baby thing is too much. Hell, he was keeping track of my menstrual cycle so he knew about when I was ovulating." She paused a moment and sat back further into her chair. "He called my cell phone when I was sleeping. He left a message and said he expected me home tonight or else. What does that mean? Or else?"

"I don't know. I don't even know what to tell you. I guess he had me totally buffaloed. Here I thought you were engaged to the perfect guy and you think I have the perfect guy. He really was keeping track of your menstrual cycle? That's crossing the line. I didn't think he was like that. He's really obsessed, isn't he? What are you going to do?"

"Yeah, I think he's getting obsessive. Maybe even a little crazy. He finally admitted the menstrual cycle thing last night. He admitted that he kept an ovulation calendar on his computer to keep track. He'd done all kinds of research to find out how to estimate when I'd be more likely to get pregnant." She giggled. "That explains the candle lit dinners once a month." Her smile faded and she looked serious. "He said that he thought we would have the most beautiful child on the earth and it was my duty to give a child to him and the world. He said it wouldn't be fair to hold something back that could bring such joy to others. He told me that our child could be the best thing to happen to the world." Jessie grunted to herself and took a sip of her wine before she continued. "Well, that's not happening. Luckily, I'd just found out my old apartment is back up for rent. My old landlord came in for some flowers a couple days ago. She was saying that she missed me and wished I'd come back. So I'm going to move back there and move on with my life. I can't let him hold me down. I mean, I have a business to run and my life to lead. It's gonna be hard for a while, I suppose, but I don't want any kids. I have decided that. I know you want me to and Sam wants me to, but you aren't the one raising the little devil. I don't think I can do it." Jessie looked at Sam for a moment and then looked back at the fire. "This whole Derik thing has been a long time coming. I mean, I expected us to have a blow out a long time ago and split apart. I'm surprised we lasted this long."

Loren was surprised and confused. "What? Then why did you stay with him if you knew it wasn't going to work? How long have you known it wouldn't work? Why didn't you ever talk to me about this before? I am your sister and we've always been there for each other. Why didn't you trust me with all of this?"

Jessie put her hands behind her head and thought for a moment. "I don't know. I guess I knew you'd have your hands full and I wasn't ready to be alone yet. But I am now and he's gonna have to except it. Seriously, I have to get away from the guy. He has dragged me down and I'm exhausted." Jessie looked at Loren. "Hey, don't look at me like that. I didn't mean to hurt you by not telling you all the bad stuff. I guess I was saving you from hearing all my troubles. Why would you want to hear all of it? It's better to just let it slide and get on with my life. You seem more broken up about the whole thing then I am. Gees Loren, I was dating the guy, not you."

Loren looked back at the fire and let the flames steal her thoughts. She was confused with her own love life and Jessie seemed to know what she wanted and had known for quite a while. Why couldn't she figure it out that easy too?

They were sisters, but seemed to be so different. Loren couldn't figure out how Jessie always knew what she wanted. She pushed through life like a football player pushing through a group of opponents, going for a touchdown. She didn't let anything stand in the way of what she wanted.

But then, as the younger sister, Loren was always confused. She could never seem to make a decision without thinking about it and then rethinking about it again. Then, with all the thinking, she usually talked herself out of half the things she wanted to do.

She looked out past the fire and admired the stars. There were thousands upon thousands of stars she could see twinkling in the clear sky and Loren sighed at the beauty of it. She looked back at Sam and Jessie and smiled. Even with all her stresses of work and home life, she was content having Sam and Jessie close to her for the moment. It was good to have them with her under the night sky. She yawned. "It is getting pretty late. I should probably head inside and get ready for bed. I have to work in the morning and it's going to be a busy."

Jessie pouted. "You can't go yet. We haven't even had marshmallows yet. I don't want to do it myself." Jessie sat up and turned towards Sam. "You don't want your mom going to bed yet, do you?"

Sam stood up, pulled the blanket around her, and went to sit on Jessie's lap. "I guess I don't care. I can stay our here with you Aunt Jessie." She tilted her head to one side and looked confused. "And what's a menstrual cycle?"

Jessie looked at Loren and then back at Sam. She had a surprised look on her face. "Oh. You heard us?"

"I'm ten. Not stupid." Sam said.

Loren shook her head. "It's not anything for you to worry about right now. It's one of those things you'll have to go through when you're older."

Sam gave Jessie a baffling look and shrugged her shoulders. "Alright. It doesn't sound like anything fun anyways. Can we have marshmallows now?"

Chapter 5

*L*oren pushed through the week and concentrated on work to forget about the other problems in her life. She had a lot of ordering and numbers to crunch before the week was over and time seemed to be getting away from her. Nonetheless, Sam begged her every day to take off so they could go to the lake or camping. But Loren needed to get done what needed to get done and a day off was going to have to wait.

Besides that, Sam never seemed too bored after spending a day at her friend Valerie's house. Loren regularly heard stories of them playing hide and go seek or occupying themselves with dolls for hours. They had dances they created and helped bake chocolate chip cookies too. After Loren picked her up, Sam would go on for fifteen minutes, or more, about all they did during the day. No, Loren wasn't worried about Sam having a bad summer or being bored.

It worked out perfect that Valerie's mom, Jodelle, stayed home during the summer and could have Sam stay there on the days Loren had to work. It gave her a sense of relief that Sam was being taken care of and with a friend of her own age. At least that was one less stress.

But Erik seemed to be on her mind a lot and she didn't know what direction to take with him. She didn't want to break off their engagement, but she didn't want him to not have a committed relationship either. She was beginning to think that she should break it off so he could pursue a relationship that might lead to marriage and a new family for him. She didn't think it was fair to keep Erik waiting. She didn't have any idea how long it would take for the marriage to happen, if it happened at all.

Maybe she was destined to remain a widower the rest of her life. Would she be heartbroken if she was? She had her chance at love and it had been good, so why try to cover it up with a new one? Would she be able to give Erik her heart like she'd given it to Craig? Was it even hers to give anymore?

Loren shuffled through some papers and pushed the thoughts to the back of her mind. Through the closed office door she heard numerous voices come into the coffee shop and decided to take a break from the papers and go help a few customers. She prided herself on giving good service to her loyal regulars and that meant getting them their coffee fresh and fast so they could enjoy it hot.

As Loren stepped from the back room she glanced at the line of customers and her eyes met glaring eyes staring back at her. It was the same red haired man, from the bar, that had been yelling at her. Loren felt the hair stand up on the back of her neck and felt a chill go down her spine. The way the man was looking at her made her feel very uneasy and protective of herself.

When he ordered his latte, he watched intently as the coffee was mixed with the milk, looking for any mistakes. Although, Loren wasn't worried about the service since she trained her staff herself and knew they knew what they were doing. It had become a science that they perfected. But still, he watched as the hot liquid filled the cup and didn't take his eyes off the process until Amber, a young lady who'd been working for Loren for two years, placed the cup on the counter in front of him. She smiled pleasantly at him and asked for the total of the purchase. He threw the money on the counter, sneered at her, and turned to leave. When he got to the door he pushed another customer aside to get through.

Amber gave a quick look at Loren and shrugged her shoulders. The man's negative demeanor didn't seem to frazzle her at all as she greeted the next customer and went to fill their order.

Loren smiled at Amber and was impressed how she responded to an irate customer. She gave the front door one more look before she turned and looked at the shop's interior. It was dark green and maroon with highlights of whites and creams to brighten it up. There were big comfy couches and chairs to rest in along with tables placed around the room too. There were shelves of books and tables of magazines for customers to enjoy, or they could bring in their own. Recently, she added Wi-Fi for the computer users and had plenty of big, fluffy pillows to be comfortable.

Loren smiled and went to fill cup dispensers and thought of the red haired man. While she worked, she couldn't help but wonder how he found his way to her store. She had never seen him there before and she'd met almost every person in the town. She wondered if he had moved here recently or just happened to come upon her shop for the first time. Even though she liked the business, he was one man she hoped would not stop back in anytime soon.

Shaking her head and grinning, Loren forgot the idea of ever seeing him again and busied herself with work until the last customer left and she locked the doors. After the floors were cleaned and everything stocked, she waved good bye to her workers and headed to her car. She got an uneasy feeling as she unlocked the door, but as she looked around she saw nothing. She was being edgy for no reason and needed to go get Sam so dinner could get started and maybe get a swim in before it got too late and the temperature plummeted.

When they got back home, Loren was surprised to see that Jessie was still at the house. She was in the kitchen and had prepared dinner consisting of spaghetti, garlic bread, and a fresh salad with onions and radishes from the garden. When Loren looked towards the living room, she could see it had been cleaned and organized. She thought Jessie was acting too casual after apparently missing work and spending the day there. She knew something was wrong.

Loren walked into the kitchen and leaned on the counter. "Hey Jessie. I didn't think you would be here when I got home. Not that anything is wrong with it, I just thought you would maybe go to work?" She looked at Jessie from top to bottom and grinned. "Are those my clothes?"

Jessie put the bread on the table and acted like it was an everyday occurrence to be fixing dinner for them. "Yes they are. I didn't feel like going anywhere today. I just figured I would take a day off and get my head straight." Jessie got a mischievous look on her face. "Hope you're okay with me borrowing clothes or I can walk around naked if you prefer," she said. Jessie smiled, but the smile faded quickly. "I mean, I know I told you last night that I knew what I was doing but, really, I have no idea. He keeps calling and calling to the point I shut my phone off. I was waiting for him to show up here. I know he knows this is where I would go. He hasn't, but I tried to keep myself busy. So you have a clean bathroom and everything is dusted. And you have a fresh cooked meal for you."

Sam sat down at the table and grabbed a piece of bread and took a big bite. "This might be a good thing for Aunt Jessie to stay here. I mean, that's less chores for me to do."

Loren smirked. "Ah, no. You'll still have chores to do. And since Aunt Jessie did the dusting, I'll have to find something else for you. It's not Jessie's job to clean our house Sammie bear."

Sam put her hands in the air and grunted. "Come on mom. Don't you know a good thing when it falls into your lap? She's being a maid. For free. Duh."

Loren and Jessie glanced at each other and couldn't help to not laugh.

Loren looked at her daughter and shook her head. "Sammie. Some days I wonder about you. How about you clean up after dinner since Aunt Jessie fixed it?"

Sam made a face and took another bite of her bread. "So Aunt Jessie, how long you staying?" She glanced at Loren. "Not to clean or anything, I guess."

Jessie sat down and filled her plate with pasta and salad. "I don't know Sammie. I guess as long as your mom lets me." She looked at Loren and pouted. "I don't have anywhere else to go right now."

Loren swallowed her bite of salad and stared at Jessie. "What about the apartment? Did you call them?"
"Well no, not exactly."

"What does that mean?" Loren asked.

"It means that I tried, but the line was busy and I didn't get around to trying again. I'll call tomorrow morning and get out of here."

Loren put her fork down and grabbed Jessie's hand. "No, that's not what I meant and you know it. I thought you had a plan, that's all. If you need to stay here, then stay here. It's no problem and there's plenty of room. We'll get some stuff organized better in the spare room and you can stay there as long as you want. We're sister's you know. I'm not throwing you out."

Jessie began to tear up and quickly looked down at her plate. "Thanks. I'd rather be with family right now." Then she pointed her finger at Sam. "And for you, I'll help with chores, but that doesn't make me a maid. Understood missy?"

Sam giggled and stuck a fork full of spaghetti into her mouth.

After cleaning the kitchen, Sam headed to her room and Loren and Jessie sat on the couch. They watched the sun set through the bay windows while Jessie was curled up in a blanket and had her feet on Loren's lap.

Loren looked away from the sunset momentarily to stare at Jessie. "So when did you want to go to your place and get your stuff? I can take the day off or if it can wait until Saturday it would be better."

Jessie shifted her direction and stared at Loren. "Have I told you how great you are lately? I mean it. You're wonderful. You always have been. Even when we were little kids you'd always be so kind and gentle with everything and everyone."

Loren ran her hands through her hair. "I don't know. I guess that's just who I am. I didn't try to be that way. It just happened. It's not always a good thing."

"I know. It's always been that way. That's why I knew you would let me stay here. Its better having your big sister around anyway, isn't it?"

"I guess we'll find out. I haven't had you around for a long time. There will be an adjustment period, I'm sure. But like I said, you're welcome to stay as long as you want. When did you want to get your stuff?"

Jessie sat up and looked out the window. "Did you hear a car door shut?"

Loren glanced out the front window and saw Erik walking towards the door. She jumped off the couch, opened the door, and gave him a hug. They held hands as they walked back into the living room and saw Jessie still sitting on the couch.

Erik leaned down and gave Jessie a hug. He smiled. "It's good to see you Jess. How have you been?"

Jessie moved over so Erik could sit down. "Oh, you know. Breaking up with the fiancé and moving in with Loren for a while."

Erik looked confused when he glanced at Loren. "She's moving in with you? How's this going to work with the wedding stuff?"

Loren sat between them, held Erik's hand, and looked into his eyes. "She's going through a rough time right now. It's no big deal."

Erik stood up like someone pinched him. He pointed his finger at Loren and spoke with a disapproving tone. "It's no big deal? You tell me you can't marry me and then your sister is moving in with you? Obviously we'll never get married. You keep making it more and more difficult. I thought we were planning on me coming here after the wedding? I guess I'm put on the back burner again."

Loren stood up and tried to touch Erik's arm and he retracted back. She was confused. "Erik, I had just told you that Sam and I didn't know if we were ready." She put her hands to her sides and giggled. "I'm sure Jessie isn't going to stay here until we are all old and gray," Loren joked and tried to lighten Erik's mood.

Erik didn't find it funny and headed to the front door. "No, she may not, but this speaks volumes about who's more important to you."

Jessie stood up, grabbed her shoes and purse and walked towards the door. Her voice was quiet when she spoke. "Hey, I didn't mean to cause any troubles. I can get a hotel room."

Loren put her hand up and stopped Jessie from walking out. "No, Jessie you're not going anywhere." She glared at Erik. "There's a big difference between my sister staying here and having another man take over as my husband and father to my child."

Erik opened the door and stepped out. "You know what Loren? I've been very patient with all of this, but I don't think you ever wanted to be married.

I think you just wanted a guy to have around when you wanted him around."

Loren didn't know what to say. She watched as Erik stormed off to his truck, slammed the door and spit gravel into the air as he sped away down the driveway.

Chapter 6

*T*he next couple of days Loren was buried in paperwork at the coffee shop. In between filing, business calls, and customers she had tried calling Erik countless times. She left him messages to call her, to forgive her, although she didn't know for what, and for him to sit down with her and talk it out. He didn't respond to one call and she was ready to throw her hands in the air with the whole relationship.

Wanting to try one last thing, she drove down to his office on her lunch break. When she stepped inside the door of his architect business, she was greeted by Georgia, his secretary. She was a short, older woman who always wore too much lipstick and perfume. She had blonde curly hair and light blue eyes that were hidden, instead of highlighted, from all the eye shadow she wore.

She had been Erik's secretary since before Loren knew him, and always greeted Loren with a smile. She would then ask if she wanted some coffee, which Loren found comical since Georgia knew she owned a coffee shop.

Loren sat down and could see Georgia's feet protruding from under the desk. Her ankles looked swollen and her shoes looked too tight as a result.

Georgia stood up from behind the desk and acted nervous. It was obvious to Loren that Erik had told her about the situation between them. Loren wondered if he mentioned it in conversation or if he whined about her every day. Either way, it made her uncomfortable, and obviously it did his secretary too.

Georgia offered her usual cup of coffee before sitting back down. "What can I do for you today, Loren? Erik isn't in right now if you came to see him. He's been out at construction sites all day."

Loren watched as she sat back in her chair and her feet slowly protruded from under the desk again. "I didn't figure I would catch him. I guess I was hoping he would drop by since its lunch time."

"Oh no. He rarely comes here at lunch. He tends to go out to eat anymore. He used to bring his lunch here, but as the company grew, I guess so did his appetite for other foods."

Loren giggled to herself. "I see. Well, could you please tell him that I stopped by and that I really think we need to talk?"

"Yes, not a problem. I'll write it down right now so I don't forget." Georgia grabbed a small notebook, with frays of paper hanging from its spine, and began to write. She didn't look up when she spoke. "I'm sorry that you two are having troubles. I know it's not my place to say anything, but I always thought you two were a good couple and I wanted it to last." Georgia moved around in her seat and looked more nervous than she originally had. She looked at Loren with sincerity. "I shouldn't have said anything. Please don't think that Erik tells me all his problems. He just mentioned it this morning. He hasn't looked to happy and I asked him why."

Loren grinned. "It's okay. You've been around for quite a while and probably know his moods better than I do. I hope we work it out. Although, I don't know quite what I did, so it makes it a little more difficult."

Georgia looked back down at her notebook. "All I know is that your sister moved in and he saw it as you not wanting to get married. Really, that's all I know."

"Again, it's okay. I'm not trying to put you in the middle of it. Just tell him I stopped by alright?"

Georgia gave Loren a concerned look and began to shuffle papers that needed to be filed. "Okay dear. I will."

Loren left the office just as confused as she was before she had gotten there. She drove back to "Good Mornings", asked to not be disturbed, and laid her head on her desk. A few minutes later, she heard a soft rapping on the door.

Amber slowly opened the door and peered inside. "Hi. I know you're having a bad day but . . . there's a guy out here causing problems. Can you come take care of it?"

Loren groaned, rolled her eyes, pushed away from her desk, and patted Amber on the back. "Let's see what's going on."

When she turned the corner to the front end of the store, she took a step back when she saw who was at the counter. It was the red haired man again. Loren mumbled to herself, "What does he want now?" She stood tall and walked behind the counter. She spoke professionally, but with a soft demeanor. "What can I do for you sir? Is there a problem?"

The man snarled his lips and spoke contemptuously. "I don't have a problem. You do!"

Loren stared at the man and tried to remain calm. "I'm sorry. Is there something wrong with your coffee or the service?"

He glared at her and leaned across the counter. "No, the coffee is tolerable. It's you I have a problem with."

Loren took a step back and noticed customers starting to watch the confrontation. "I'm sorry sir. I really don't know what I could've done to make you feel that way."

"You know damn well why I have a problem. You, the bar, and you're mouth. I think the people in this place need to know how you really are. I don't think they should be under the false pretense that you're sweet and nice."

Loren stepped back towards the counter and met his gaze. "Sir, this is my shop. I don't appreciate you coming in here making such allegations about me or disrupting my customers' quiet afternoon. If you want to talk we can go outside and sit. Or I can call the police for you disturbing my place of business. Which would you prefer?"

The man's shoulders dropped and he looked calmer. "Fine. Let's take this outside then."

Loren glanced at Amber and gave her a concerned look. Amber nodded her head, as if she understood, and grabbed a cordless phone. She followed Loren and man to the opened door and stood there, making sure she didn't have to call for help.

Loren peeked back at Amber and was reassured that she was close by. Then she sat at a table, right next to the doorway, and waited to see if the man would join her.

He sat down and banged his fist on the table, making the metal underneath vibrate. He shook his finger in her face. "You. You are not a nice person. I think people should know that. I met the real you, didn't I?"

Loren sat back in her seat and took a big breath and then exhaled it loudly. "Sir. I really am sorry for the other night. I was having a bad day and you happened to be there when my frustrations spilled out. No, that is not who I am. I don't go around screaming at people or picking fights. It was simply a bad night. I'm sorry."

He stared at her. It took him a few seconds before he could speak again. "Oh. I wasn't expecting a response like that. I . . . I was expecting you to get into my face, screaming."

Loren grinned. "Sorry if I ruined your plans. I actually don't like confrontations and would rather smile all day if I could."

He folded his arms in front of him and had a confused look on his face. He furrowed his eyebrows and then tried to smile. "Well then . . . I guess I owe you an apology."

Loren raised her eyebrows. "That's it? You cause an uproar in my store and can calm down that fast? Not that I'm complaining but . . ."

"Yeah, I know. My barks worse than my bite. It's bothered me the last few days since I saw you in here the last time. I've never had a woman stand up to me like you did, and I didn't know how to react to it. Maybe it's the red hair," he said and tugged at the hair at the top of his head. "I now know I reacted totally wrong. I'm sorry. I'm Cody, by the way."

Loren looked back to see Amber staring in disbelief. Amber shrugged her shoulders and smiled before taking a step back and sat down in a chair, still within listening distance.

Loren turned back and laughed. "I'm sorry Cody. I just find this all to be crazy."

"Well, I got your heart pumping huh? Let's start over. Can I get your name?"

"It's Loren. My name is Loren." She pointed inside the store. "And that is Amber."

"Looks like you have some pretty good employees. I guess I'd be scared if a crazy man like me came in too." He waved to Amber and spoke towards her. "Sorry Amber."

Amber waved back, then looked away but remained seated.

Loren didn't know what to do or say. She had never been in a situation like this one. It was extremely awkward. When she looked back towards Cody, he seemed to be lost in his own thoughts and was staring at the table. Loren said, "So . . . how did you happen to find my shop anyways?"

Cody scratched his head. He looked up at Loren and looked confused. "Huh. I really don't know. I'm sure I heard it from one of the guys at work, but I can't be sure." He paused a moment. "No. I know where I heard about it. I was at the grocery store waiting in line and a couple of gals were talking about coming here to sit down and have an espresso. They were talking about how comfortable it was and how they felt like they could sit here for hours. I figured if they thought it was that good, that I should give it a try." He looked at Loren and grinned. "Then I see you walk around the corner and I couldn't believe it. I feel dumb now from the way I acted the first time and how I was today."

"Well, we're okay now right? So it's water under the bridge."

Cody didn't respond. He stared back at the table and tapped his foot on the ground.

Loren was happy they settled things, but she was growing impatient. She still had a lot of work to do. "So are we done here?" Loren asked.

Cody stood up and put his hand out to help Loren to her feet. "Yeah, we're done here. Again, I'm sorry. Do you want me to apologize to your customers?"

Loren accepted Cody's hand and stood up next to him. She looked inside her shop and smiled. "No. That's the great thing about this town. It's small enough that you feel safe, but big enough that people don't dwell on the gossip. Did you just move here?" she asked as she took a step closer to the shop door.

"Yep. I transferred here a few weeks ago to work at the power plant. I hope you're right about the gossip thing."

"Nah, everyone pretty much keeps to themselves. I mean there has been a few stories, but no one cares about little things." She smiled. "Like a man acting crazy in a coffee shop."

"Ha-ha. Very funny. I feel pretty foolish. I guess I just felt I needed to protect my reputation, even though I haven't started a good one with you."

"Your fine Cody. Next time just come in for a cup of coffee, okay?"

"It's a deal," he said and turned to walk down the sidewalk.

Loren waited until he walked around the corner before she turned back towards Amber. "Can you believe that? What a day I'm having. Thanks for having my back."

Amber followed her to the counter and placed the phone down. "I thought I was gonna have to call the cops. You handled that like a pro. I'm impressed."

Loren patted Amber on the back. "You learn with age. And keeping a level head helped too. I'm actually impressed with myself. I was getting a little scared, to tell you the truth."

"What did you tell him to get him so mad in the first place?" Amber asked.

"Honestly, I couldn't even tell you. I was having a rough day and he happened to be at the wrong place at the wrong time."

Amber raised her eyebrows with surprise. "Remind me to never get on your bad side," she said before strolling down the counter to get a customer a refill.

Loren headed back to her office and stayed there until it was closing time. She said a few quick goodbyes and headed home. She was excited that Jessie had stayed home with Sam which made one less stop. She didn't want to have to converse or think for the rest of the night. All she wanted to do was to relax, take a hot bath, and go to bed.

When Loren opened the front door, she was blown away with the sound of loud music. She walked into the living room to see Jessie and Sam dancing and turning in circles. At first she was tempted to yell at them to turn it down, but then she decided it would be more fun to join them. So she dropped her purse onto the floor, grabbed Sam's hands, and turned in circles. They spun and spun until they were both dizzy and fell to the couch laughing.

Jessie fell on top of them and all three laughed until their sides hurt and had tears in their eyes.

Finally, Jessie got up, turned down the volume, and fell back onto the couch. "What a day."

Loren wiped her eyes and enjoyed the release of tension from a good laugh. "What about your day? It looked pretty good to me."

Sam interrupted. "Oh it was. We blew bubbles outside, jumped on the beds, had a pillow fight, and . . . oh yeah, we rollerbladed in the hallway."

Jessie put her hand over Sam's mouth. "Stop. You're gonna get me in trouble."

Loren grinned at Sam and then tried to give Jessie an angry look. "You rollerbladed on my hallway floor?"

"Oh, we didn't hurt it. I checked," Jessie answered. "Hey, we made you dinner. We fixed breakfast for dinner. We made . . ."

Sam interjected, "Let me tell her Aunt Jessie. We made Apple Puff Pancakes, bacon, and a fruit salad. Does it sound good mommy? Can you smell it? It just got done a few minutes ago."

Loren sniffed the air and could smell the apples and bacon. "Smells delicious. Let's eat."

Sam followed her into the kitchen but then cut in front of her to grab a piece of bacon. "I helped make it all," she said proudly.

Loren looked over at Jessie and nodded her head approvingly. She smiled. "Good job Sammie bear. At least *she* can get you to cook."

They filled their plates and sat at the table. A few minutes went by before anyone spoke. Sam was first. "So, how was your day mom?"

"Let's just say it wasn't as good as yours. But having a nice dinner and such a beautiful daughter to look at makes it better."

"Thanks mom. Oh, we also went to the store and got a bunch of boxes for Aunt Jessie's stuff. They're in the garage."

Loren looked at Jessie and frowned. "Oh yeah, tomorrow is the day huh? That's gonna be a good day too. I hope we can fit it all in our vehicles."

"Why don't you ask to use Erik's truck? I bet he'd let you," Sam chimed in.

Loren gave Jessie a quick glance before she looked at Sam. "Oh, I don't think that would be such a good idea right now."

"Why?" Sam asked.

Jessie touched Sam's arm and frowned. "Well, Sammie, it's kind of tough right now. Your mom and Erik are kind of having a little fight."

"Why?" Sam asked again. She took her last bite of fruit salad and stopped chewing for a second, lost in thought. She finished chewing as fast as she could and looked at Loren. "Is it because I said I didn't want you to get married?" She looked like she was on the verge of tears before she finished her sentence.

"Oh no baby. It's not that. We're arguing about something else," Loren said as she walked around the table to sit next to Sam.

Sam choked back her tears. "I know it is. I told him no and now you two are breaking up. I didn't mean it. I just wanted time to . . ."

Loren wrapped Sam into her arms and hugged her tight. "Sammie bear, it's not your fault. Don't ever think that. He's mad at me for something else. It has nothing to do with what you said. You did nothing wrong. You have to say how you feel. I'm proud of you how you talked to Erik the other day. It was very grown up."

Jessie kneeled next to Sam and hugged them both. "Sammie, don't worry your pretty little head about it. It's my fault, not yours."

Loren frowned at Jessie. "It's no one's fault. It was simply miscommunication. Now, I don't want to hear you say that either Jessie. And that's the end of it. Now I want to enjoy my meal, take a bath, and watch a movie in bed. Who's up for watching a movie with me?"

Chapter 7

*J*essie and Loren both scanned the area around the house to try and see if Derik was home. Carrying boxes with them, they quietly opened the front door and went inside. Jessie walked through the house, to see if Derik was there, and gave Loren a thumbs up to say they were alone. Frantically, they began to pile Jessie's belongings into the boxes, not saying a word.

Loren glanced around the house and could remember so many happy times there. They had celebrated Christmas's and Thanksgiving's, along with a couple birthdays in their house. Besides that, Loren had helped them paint almost every room and had helped Jessie set up their entertainment center. But now the house looked daunting. It had become something else in a matter of a few days to Loren.

She glanced in the kitchen and saw a drawing that Sam had done for them. It was a picture of Jessie and Derik getting married and they had a small dog and cat at their side. It had taken Sam a couple hours to work on the picture and Loren definitely wasn't going to let it stay here with Derik. So after taping the box shut she was working on, she stepped over it and grabbed the picture. Carefully, she rolled it up and placed it in her purse.

After a dozen boxes were filled and taped shut, Loren stood up and stretched her back. "Jess, you have a lot of stuff. I don't think we're gonna fit it all in our two vehicles."

"Oh yes we will. And what we don't fit will stay here and he can do with it as he pleases."

"But Jess. You can't leave these things," Loren whined as she pointed to Jessie's couch and love seat. She remembered being with Jessie to pick them out. They had such a good day of shopping and then she decided to get the chairs as a present to Derik.

"Yes I can. And I will. Now, quit talking and get to packing," Jessie said as she threw a handful of DVD's into a box.

Loren shook her head and began to move boxes outside to her Jeep. Each time she ducked into the Jeep, or back out, she would glance around to make sure Derik wasn't coming down the street. She continued to move boxes until both their vehicles were piled as high as the ceiling and no room was left on the floors.

As they moved the last lamp out, they both sighed with relief. They had packed everything, except for the couch and love seat. Although, Loren planned on finding a pick-up to borrow and was going to get them herself if she needed to. She wasn't going to have Jessie buy new things just because of Derik. She didn't care if it was a present for him or not. Jessie had spent her money on them and he didn't deserve something so nice from her.

As Loren slammed her door, she glanced up and saw Derik coming around the corner in his black pick-up truck. Loren quickly grabbed Jessie's arm and pushed her inside her SUV and told her to leave.

Derik slammed on his brakes, slammed his door, and ran towards Jessie. Before she could put her SUV into drive, he swung open her door and grabbed her arm. He yanked until she was screaming and forced her to get out of the car.

Loren pulled on his arm and began to plead with him. "Let her go. You need to let her arm go. You're hurting her!"

Derik glared at Loren. "You keep your mouth shut. I'm sure you had something to do with this. You always act like she belongs to you." He tightened his grip on Jessie. "She's mine!" he yelled.

Jessie started to kick at Derik and struggled to free herself. "Let me go! It's over between us. Get over it!"

Derik grabbed her other arm and squeezed hard. He glared at her and spoke contemptuously. "Look here Jessie. We're going inside the house and talk this out. You owe me that. But you're not leaving until you see my point of view and see that we're supposed to be together and have a family."

Jessie grimaced from the pain. "I'm not having your baby. Don't you get it? I don't want kids. Not with you or anyone. Now, let me go!"

He ignored what Jessie said and started to pull her towards the house, kicking and screaming.

Loren knew she couldn't let them get there. It would be a bad situation to have Jessie cornered and knew she had to stop him. Not knowing what else to do, she jumped on Derik's back. She started to scream at him to let Jessie go and punched at him wherever her fist would hit.

Derik let one of Jessie's arms free and began to fight back. He smacked at the air, trying to connect with any part of Loren that he could.

Loren dodged his hand and continued to punch at him and then dug her nails into his shoulders. He started to jump around.

Loren held on like she was on a bucking bronco. She knew if she fell, he could hurt her worse.

He continued to hold Jessie's arm and swung with his other hand. Finally, his hand connected with Loren's face. She could feel blood gush from her nose, but she wasn't going to let go.

Derik edged towards the house and didn't stop until he heard sirens approaching. "Great! Look what you did!"

Loren jumped from his back as a police officer sprang from his car and had his hand positioned on his gun. He continually asked Derik to let Jessie go so the situation didn't get any more out of control.

Derik ignored the officer's demands and held tight to Jessie. He continued to drag her towards the front door of the house. "She's mine. Don't you get it? She's mine," he half pleaded and half screamed at the officer.

Another cruiser came around the corner and screeched to a halt. The second officer was a bigger man, but moved quickly beside the first officer. He pointed a stun gun at Derik. Loren heard him yell countless times that he didn't want to Taser him, but he would if he didn't let her go.

Derik cursed at him.

Jessie was screaming from the pain in her arms and yelling for the officer to shoot him.

Then, quick as lightning, Loren saw Derik release Jessie and then he was on the ground. He seemed momentarily paralyzed from the stun gun that had connected with his hip. He began to make noises from the electrical current going through is body along with no control of his movements. Finally, it subsided and he laid there like he was comatose.

Jessie ran to Loren and buried her face on Loren's shoulder. She sobbed uncontrollably and had a hard time catching her breath. She held on to Loren tightly before she finally slid down to the ground. She sat with her arms around her legs, hugging them, rocking back and forth.

Loren kneeled beside her and hugged her tight. She glanced up to see the officers put handcuffs on Derik and couldn't help but to smile to herself. They placed him inside one of the cruiser's and she could hear him pleading for Jessie to tell them it was all a misunderstanding. He yelled for her to help him until the door was shut and his words became muffled.

They heard more sirens, as an ambulance came in front of the house too. A paramedic led Jessie to sit down at the back of the ambulance so they could look at her arms. Another paramedic dabbed the blood from Loren's nose and told her she would be okay.

"Loren, I want to go home. Can we go home?" Jessie pleaded.

"Oh Jessie." Loren sat down beside her and tried to comfort her the best she could. She knew they would be there until their story was documented by the police. "I'll get us home as soon as I can. We can't go right now, but we will soon. I promise." Loren held back tears as she spoke and watched as they placed ice packs on Jessie's arms. She listened as they told her it was severe bruising and would be better in a couple weeks.

Suddenly, Loren looked at her watch and had a feeling of panic. She was supposed to pick Sam up an hour ago. Trying not to distress Jessie anymore, Loren walked to the front of the ambulance and called Jodelle. She explained some of the situation and said she would be there as soon as she could. Jodelle was very understanding and told her the girls' were just fine. She said to take her time and do what she needed first. Hanging up, Loren took a deep breath, walked back to Jessie, and gave her a big hug.

When they finally got back home, after Jessie assured her that she could drive, Loren grabbed an ice pack and helped Jessie to the couch. She covered her with a blanket and gave her a kiss on top of her head. "Sis. I'm so sorry this happened. Maybe we should've waited a few more days."

"Oh Loren. You know as well as I do that it doesn't matter how much time we would've waited. He would've done the same thing. Now, go get my niece. I want a hug from her."

Loren tried to smile, but she was worried. "I can stay here a while first."

"I'm fine. I'm really tired and want to take a short nap. Just make sure you lock the door when you leave, okay?"

"Okay Jess. I'll go get Sammie. I'll be back soon. You have your cell phone if you need me, right?"

"Quit worrying. It's over and he can't get to me from jail."

Sam started asking questions from the moment she got inside the car. When they got home, she ran through the door and jumped on the couch. "Aunt Jessie, you don't look that bad."

Jessie removed the ice pack from her left arm and showed it to Sam.

Sam's eyes instantly filled with tears. "Oh my gosh. How could he be so mean?"

Loren hugged Sam and looked at Jessie sympathetically. "She'll heal up in no time at all. We don't know why he did this. I guess everyone has a mean streak in them."

Sam sat next to Jessie and gently kissed her arm. "That was a magic kiss. It'll heal faster now.

Chapter 8

After putting extra items into the basement, Loren and Jessie fell back onto the bed exhausted. It had only taken a couple hours before the spare room already exhibited Jessie's personality. It didn't even look like a spare room at all. It looked like Jessie had been there for years.

Loren looked at some of the art work on the walls then turned her gaze towards the heaping full closet. "Dang, how much shopping do you do in a year? We put at least three big boxes down stairs with clothes in them too. You're going to let me borrow some of this, aren't you?"

"Not before me," Sam chimed in as she came into the room and fell into the closet. She sat on the floor and wrapped the hanging clothes around her head. "You have much better stuff then mom does."

"Hey, I resent that comment," Loren giggled.

Jessie rested her head on top of Loren's stomach and stared at the ceiling. "I think we did a pretty good job. It only took us three days to finally start."

"I don't know why I had to help to start out with. It's not my things," Loren said teasingly. "Besides that, you couldn't help a few days ago and I wasn't going to do it myself."

"Hey, what am I? Chopped liver?" Sam hollered from the closet.

"Yeah, thanks for the help," Jessie said and raised her arms in the air to inspect the ugly colored bruises. She turned her wrists to see that the bruises went all the way around both of her arms.

Loren winced when she saw the bruises. "Hey, those are healing quicker than I thought. You won't even see them in a week. Are they still tender?"

"Ah, yeah. I can barely take a shower. Just the pressure from the water hurts. I'm gonna be taking baths for a while, I think."

"I suppose you could use the tub in my room. Since it is bigger than the other one," Loren uttered softly.

"Is that a fat joke?" Jessie giggled.

Loren laughed. "Yeah, you're so huge Jess. Gees. I don't think I'll be able to fit into some of your clothes since you're so tiny."

Sam grabbed a pair of three inch stilettoes and began to put them on. "I bet I could fit into them," she said as she tightened the straps around her ankles. She tried to stand up and her ankles turned in as soon as she put weight on them. She glanced towards the bed to see if they were watching her and quickly sat down to take the shoes back off. "Umm. I think I'll try to find a pair that's not so tall.

Loren and Jessie stared at each other and tried not to laugh. Instead, Loren pushed Jessie from her stomach and sat on the floor next to Sam. "Don't try to grow up too fast. I want to keep you my baby as long as I can."

Sam put her head on Loren's shoulder. "I'm not a baby, mom. I'm ten years old. Only eight or nine more years and I will be living on my own."

"Don't remind me," Loren groaned. "Anyways, I need to get to work. I wasn't expecting for us to decorate your room too. They probably think I was kidnapped or something. I'm surprised the military hasn't crashed down the doors yet."

Sam rolled her eyes. "Ah mom. Stop being so dramatic."

Loren stood up, rolled her shoulders, and headed down the stairs. "Don't get into too much trouble. And there will be *no*, I repeat *no*, rollerblading in the house," she hollered as she grabbed her purse and headed out the door.

As Loren stepped inside "Good Mornings" she noticed Cody sitting at a table next to the counter. She tried to quietly walk behind him and sneak towards her office.

Alex, another employee, shook his head at her. "Good morning. There is a gentleman waiting for you," he said loudly.

Loren glared at Alex and saw Cody turn towards the counter.

He said, "Hey there. I've been waiting for you. Can you join me for a cup of your coffee?"

"Hello Cody. I didn't see you there," she fibbed. "I got in late and need to get busy with some paperwork. Can I get a rain check?"

"Well, you're already late so what's another few minutes?" Cody asked.

Loren turned her back towards him and took a deep breath. She filled a cup with her favorite blend of coffee and nudged Alex. She whispered, "How long has he been here?"

Alex pretended to wipe the counter and stood shoulder to shoulder with Loren. "He's been here for two hours and three lattes."

"He's persistent," Loren whispered before she turned to sit down with Cody.

Cody leaned back in his chair as Loren sat down. He took a sip from his coffee and sighed. "I never thought you'd get here. The kid behind the counter said you'd be in, but I started to wonder."

"I'm sorry for making you wait. What can I do for you?"

Cody let out another sigh before he spoke. "Oh, I just thought we could talk on good terms for once."

Loren gave him a confused look. "You've been waiting here to have a civilized conversation?"

"Pretty much. I had the day off and thought of you."

"You thought of me?" Loren asked and pointed to herself. "Why?"

"I don't know. I guess you sparked my curiosity. You puzzle me and I wanted to get to know you a little better. Is that okay?"

Loren leaned back in her chair. "Okay? I guess. So what do you want to talk about?"

Cody rubbed his chin with his hand. "I don't know."

Loren giggled. "You've been sitting here all this time and don't know what you want to talk about?"

"No, I guess not," Cody answered.

"All right, how about your job? How's that going?"

"I guess it's a good place to work and you were right about the gossip thing. I haven't heard any since I started there. Not even any rumors of a crazy guy yelling in a coffee shop."

Loren grinned and rolled her eyes. "Good. I told you it's a decent town. So . . . did you buy a house or renting somewhere?"

"Well, I'm renting right now, but have my eye on a place a few blocks from here. It's an old Victorian style house and I really like it. Although, I need to get inside to see how much work there is to it. Those old houses can cost you if you don't know what you're looking for. How about you? You live here in town?"

"No. I have an acreage a ways from here. I wanted to enjoy the scenery of Montana. It's quite beautiful."

"Huh. Sounds nice. Any kids?"

Loren wrinkled her forehead. "Why?"

"No reason. Just asking. Is that okay?"

"Yeah, you're fine. It just caught me off guard. I have a little girl. Well, not so little anymore, but still my little girl. How about you?"

"Nope. No kids for me. I've been engaged twice, but they both ended. Well, obviously. I just haven't found the right one I guess." He paused. "How long you owned this place?" he asked and took another sip from his coffee.

"My husband and I started it up four years ago. It was pretty disgusting when we bought it, but he said he saw potential in it. So, I took his word for it. He was right," Loren said and looked around at the comfy couches and chairs along with tables placed sporadically.

Cody shuffled in his chair and looked embarrassed. "Your husband, huh. I'm sorry. I didn't see a ring on your hand so I just assumed." He took another quick sip of coffee and looked around the shop. Almost like he was expecting to see Loren's husband watching him.

"Hey, you're okay. My husband passed away a few years ago."

Cody leaned forward. "Again, I'm sorry."

"I don't go around announcing it to people, so you have nothing to be sorry for. I just stopped wearing my ring a couple years ago. I don't know if it's the right thing now or not," she said and thought of Erik.

"Oh. I wasn't hitting on you. I . . ."

"No. I wasn't talking about you. I was thinking about . . . oh, never mind."

"So, was he a good guy?"

Loren let her memories of Craig flood her mind. "My husband? Yes, he was the best of the best. He was my everything and then some. He could make me happy on my worst days and made me laugh all the time. He was my soul mate. And every time I step into this place, I feel him here. He had put in so many hours to make it just right and painted every wall."

"Wow. Sounds like a pretty tight relationship. How'd he die, if you don't mind me asking?"

"Don't know for sure."

Cody sat back in his chair again and stared. "What do you mean?"

"He went off the side of a mountain. From what was left, they couldn't figure out if he fell asleep, lost control, or tried to dodge something. It had started raining before they found him so there were no tracks or skid marks to figure it out."

"Oh, that's horrible. I'm sorry."

"Thank you, but I've tried to come to terms with it."

"I couldn't imagine. It looks like you have turned out pretty good since then. I mean that you are in good spirits. Was the other night because of all of it?"

Loren laughed. "The other night was about a guy I've been dating and everything else. It was a bad night, as you found out."

"I've tried to put that behind me. I definitely misjudged you. What about this other guy? What did he do?"

Loren glanced at Cody and her thoughts began to stray. She thought about sitting with him with a cup of coffee and she liked the feeling of being comfortable talking to him. She didn't know if that was a good thing or not. Was she cheating on Erik talking to another guy?

Erik didn't seem to care about anything right now. He seemed self-absorbed in what he wanted and not what she needed. She was confused about all of it.

She knew he was a good guy, but maybe not the right guy for her. But, then again, he made her laugh and smile. He consoled her when she was hurting and was patient with her. He tried to be there for her and tried to make Sam happy too. But, now, sitting with Cody, it seemed relaxed. Even easy to talk to him. She wished Erik was this easy going.

"Hello?" Cody waved his hand in front of Loren's face.

Loren blushed. "Oh, sorry. I got lost in my thoughts. Hey, it's been nice talking to you, but I really need to get to work."

"You're funny. I had just said that I'd let you get going, but obviously you didn't hear me."

Loren rubbed her temples and felt a headache coming through. "Sorry again."

"Don't be. Would you want to do this again sometime?" He touched her hand. "Only as friends. And I mean, just friends."

Loren grinned and actually liked the idea. "Sure. Come back in anytime or maybe I'll look you up. Wait, you're new in town. Got a phone number?"

Cody wrote his number on a napkin and stood up to leave. "I'll see you around, Loren."

Loren waved good bye and headed back to her office. Alex gave her a funny look as she walked by him, but she didn't have to explain herself to him or anyone else.

Chapter 9

*T*he next weekend Loren wanted to do absolutely nothing work related. She wanted to watch some movies, swim, and eat. That was it. But, of course, she got a call from the shop that a steam wand was clogged and they couldn't fix it. So, she had to go into town for a couple hours and fix that and then decided to finish up on some paperwork while she was there.

When she finally got back home, she wanted to cry. First, Jessie had brought Sam's friend Valerie to the house and the two girls were running around screaming about some make believe ghosts that were chasing them. Then, Jessie decided to try her hand at baking and made an absolute mess in the kitchen. Lastly, when Loren finally sat down to try and relax, her phone rang. It was Erik. He asked if he could come out to talk.

What was she to do? She couldn't tell him no. He already had misconceptions and she didn't want it to get worse. So, she told him the house was a mess and Sam had a friend over however he was still welcome if he wanted. She hoped he would say it could wait, but he said he was on his way.

Loren went to sit in the kitchen while she waited. Jessie took some cookies out of the oven and Loren's stomach grumbled when she smelled their sweetness. "Jess, you sure made a mess although the results look wonderful. Can I have one please?"

Jessie put a cookie on a plate and handed it to Loren. She also grabbed a glass and got her some milk to go with it. "Have a rough morning sis?"

"You could say that. Erik is on his way over here too."

"Oh. You want me to take the girls outside for a while?"

"That sounds tempting, but maybe I need witnesses around." She took a bite of the hot cookie and moaned. "This hits the spot."

Jessie grabbed herself a cookie and leaned on the counter. "You don't need witnesses. Erik's not like Derik."

"How do you know? Did you know Derik would freak out like he did?"

"Well, no. But he has a different personality than Erik."

"Yeah. Well, I didn't expect Erik to get so mad about you staying here. Maybe neither of us know him as well as we think either."

"Ah, come one Loren. That was just miscommunication. You'll work it out with him. That is, if you want to." She stared at Loren. "Do you want to?"

Loren enjoyed her cookie and ignored the question.

Jessie grabbed another cookie and tore of a chunk to let it cool. "I repeat. Do you want to?"

Loren exhaled. "I don't know anymore. Maybe I should stay single. Maybe I should just concentrate on Sammie and forget men all together. Maybe . . ."

The doorbell rang.

Loren jumped. "I don't want to do this."

Jessie touched Loren's arm and grinned at her. "It'll be fine. I'm gonna take the girls for a walk and try to find some pretty wild flowers. Don't worry. We won't stray that far from the house." She stepped around the corner and yelled up the stairs. "Girls. Let's go for a walk."

Sam and Valerie came stomping down the stairs, laughing the entire way. They put on their shoes and headed out the patio door leading to the back yard.

The doorbell rang again.

"Ah, you going to answer that?" Jessie asked as she slipped on her shoes.

"Oh. Sorry," Loren said and walked to open the door.

Jessie giggled. "You're out of it." She left through the patio door and grabbed the girls' hands and took off running through the backyard.

Loren watched them for a moment before she went to open the front door.

Erik had a confused look on his face. "I was wondering if you were going to answer." He walked into the house and looked around. Sarcastically he said, "Where's your sister?"

Loren closed her eyes and took a deep breath. This wasn't starting out very well. "They went for a walk to give us some privacy. Want to sit on the couch?"

Nodding his head, Erik strolled to the living room. He sat down and patted the cushion for her to sit next to him.

Loren suddenly felt uncomfortable and shy. Nonetheless, she sat down anyways and fidgeted with her hands in her lap.

Erik turned his body towards her and crossed his legs. "Loren, I've done a lot of thinking. I think I jumped to conclusions and should've listened to what happened first. My friend down at the station told me what happened with Derik. Is Jessie alright?"

Loren wondered if he really cared or if he was embarrassed for not knowing the facts. "Yeah, she's fine. She has some bruises and bad memories, but she'll survive. She's a strong woman."

"And you? I heard you got whacked in the nose."

"I'm fine. It stopped bleeding before the paramedics left."

"Why didn't you call me to help you move stuff?"

Loren raised her eyebrows and looked at him surprised. "Really? You have to ask that?"

"Hey, I would've helped out."

"I don't think so."

Erik looked hurt. "Now Loren, that's not fair. I'm not a heartless guy. I would 've helped under the circumstances."

Loren was irritated. "We handled it just fine. Is that why you came to talk to me?"

"Gees Loren. You're making this hard. You don't have to be so cynical with me."

"What do you expect? I mean, really. You storm out of here without hearing all the details, and now you tell me you're not heartless and a good guy." Loren stood up and her heart begin to pump hard. "I've been going through a tough time with all of this. I know you said you were patient, but you've never gone through what I did. And, frankly, I don't think you've been that patient. You've never had the love of your life die and not be able to say good bye to him. You've never had to open yourself back up again." Loren started to pace the room and began to feel claustrophobic in her own house. "Believe it or not, this is hard for me. It's not just me I have to think about. I have to know that this is right for Sam too. I have to know that she won't get hurt or push you away." She stomped her foot and looked at Erik. "Damn it. This is not easy for me. Craig helped build this house. We made love in my bedroom. We laughed in the kitchen and cooked together. We bought the furniture together and cuddled up to watch the fire for hours. He is everywhere I go. He is at my work, he is here, and he is everywhere. I loved him so much!"

Erik sat still and did not say a word. He looked stunned.

Loren stared at him for a second longer before she fell on the couch beside him and exhaled noisily. "Erik, I love you. I really do. I'm just so confused. I don't know if I can move on. I wasn't planning on starting a new life with someone else. I think you are the right man to start with, but that doesn't make it any easier."

Erik rubbed his temples. "I don't know what to do either. Do I wait for you to figure it out or do I throw a year's worth of love into the garbage?" He looked at Loren lovingly. "Loren, I knew from the start that this wouldn't be easy. I knew about Craig and your relationship. I'm not trying to be him. I could never be him. If you love me, then you'll accept me for me and try to move on with me. If you love me, like you say, then you'll know that Craig's memory might always be there, but that is what it is now. A memory." He took a deep breath and ran his hand through his hair. "I love you Loren. I love Sam. I love both of you and want you both in my life forever. I want to create new memories with you in this house. I want to sit in front of the fire with you. Not like you and Craig did but like you and I can. If you want to buy new furniture to make things easier, then we can. Or we can leave it as it is. Hell, if you want to buy a new house, we can. Loren, I'm trying so hard. Can't you see that?"

Loren felt tears well up and she tried to push them away. She didn't want to be the sappy woman.

She didn't want to cry all the time. She wanted to be happy.

She stared into Erik's eyes and had the sensation of butterflies in her stomach. She knew she was in love with him. She knew she wanted a life with him. Why couldn't she let Craig go?

Loren threw her arms around Erik and kissed him passionately. She drew back for a moment and looked into his eyes again. "I want us to be together. I really do." She kissed him again and liked that he held her in his arms.

She pushed him back on the couch and was laying on top of him. She put her hands under his head so she could kiss him with even more passion. Then tears suddenly began to fall down her cheeks. She ignored them.

Erik gently pushed her away. "What's wrong?" he asked and wiped the tears from her face.

"I'm overwhelmed."

Erik sat up and held her in his arms. "Loren, it will come in time. If it's meant to be then it's meant to be." He stroked her hair. "I'm sorry for getting so upset the other day. I guess I was hurt more by Sam not wanting us to get married then I thought."

Loren sat up straight and turned her body towards him. "That's just it though. She told me she wants us to get married. She's just afraid that she'll forget her dad."

Erik smiled. "She said that? I mean the getting married part?"

"Yes she did. She's just as confused as me with Craig's memory. We both want to start new memories, but don't want to lose the old ones. Does that make sense?"

"Unfortunately it does. So I'm back to thinking, where does that leave me?"

Loren gave him a hug and didn't let go. She whispered, "Please don't give up on us. We both love you. We just need time to figure out the rest."

Erik pulled back and stared into Loren's eyes. "You promise?"

"I promise."

Erik kissed Loren sweetly and then with more desire. Within moments he began to breathe heavily and pulled her tightly to him. He ran his hands down her back softly.

Loren liked the feel of it. She responded with kissing him back hard. She felt the heat intensify and hoped Jessie would stay on a walk for a while longer. She suddenly had the urge to be with him and wanted to satisfy the urge immediately.

She pushed Erik back on the couch again and ran her hand up and down his thigh. She wanted to feel closer to him than she had ever been before. She wanted to feel his heat penetrate against her skin. She wanted to experience his touch in new ways.

Shaking her head to herself, she knew that couldn't happen right now with Jessie and the girls so close to the house. So she settled for the next best thing. She held him tight and kissed him passionately, feeling him respond to her movements and touch. She knew he wanted the same thing she did. Loren was tempted to sneak upstairs and fall on the bed together, but the thought of the girls walking back into the house made the idea too risky.

Erik brushed his hand through her hair and she liked the tingly sensation it gave her. She closed her eyes and enjoyed every moment she was experiencing with him. The heat from his hands made her flesh hot while the pressure of him pushing against her was making her go crazy.

Loren wanted to rip his clothes off and feel his naked body beside her. She wanted to feel him within her and to explode from the excitement. Loren heard herself moan from just the thought and pulled Erik even closer. The room seemed to spin and the moans and heat seemed to make her feel intoxicated.

Erik moved his hands down her side and grabbed her hips. Then he moved them back up towards her breasts and stopped just inches from them. He teased her by moving his hands up and down her stomach and grazing his fingertips on the tops of her breasts.

Loren couldn't control herself anymore and began to gasp and started to unbutton his shirt and pants. She unzipped his pants and then suddenly heard laughter in the distance. She shook her head and began to button his shirt again. "I can't do this right now. Not with them walking into the house any second."

Erik closed his eyes and took a deep breath. "It was just getting good." He ran his hand through his hair and finished buttoning his shirt and jeans. "We'll have to finish this sometime soon," he whispered in her ear and sat up.

"I know. I want that too," Loren said. She gave him a small kiss and went to the bathroom to check her makeup and hair. When she came out she gave Erik a quick glance to make sure that he looked alright too.

Just as they sat at the table with a glass of water, Loren looked out the patio door and could see Jessie and the girls heading back to the house. Each girl had a hand full of flowers and Loren got up to find a vase. She glanced at Erik. "They're already on their way back. That was cutting it close."

Erik laughed and shook his head. "Loren, I'm sure they won't know anything happened. So quit worrying."

Sam and Valerie came into the house laughing and holding on to each other's hand. Sam looked at Erik and then at Loren. "I didn't know you were here Erik. When did you get here?"

Erik smiled. "Oh, a while ago. You were already gone. Those are some pretty flowers. Your mom got a vase for them."

Sam gave Erik a weird look. "I thought Aunt Jessie said that you guys weren't getting along? Are you now?"

Erik glanced up at Loren and back at Sam. "I guess you could say that."

Sam shrugged her shoulders and gave her flowers to Loren. "Do you like them mom? Valerie wanted to know if she could bring hers back to her own house though."

Loren took Sam's flowers and put them in the vase. She put Valerie's in a paper bag and set them in the refrigerator. "Not a problem" She looked at Valerie and smiled. "Are you going to give them to your mom? I bet she would really love them."

Valerie jumped up onto a stool next to the counter. She stared at the cookies. "Yeah. She likes flowers. Umm, can I have a cookie?"

"Yes, you can. I made them for you girls," Jessie said as she closed the door behind her. She looked at Loren and then at Erik and back at Loren again. She got a huge smile on her face. "Looks like you two made up. Good thing I took the girls for a walk, huh Loren?"

Loren blushed. "We just talked Jess."

Jessie smirked. "Yeah, just talked. Right."

Chapter 10

*I*t was a beautiful evening to sit outside. Loren watched as a hawk let the wind carry it on its breeze as it looked for a meal for the night. She continued admiring it, fascinated by its beauty and strength. She thought about how it could look so stunning to the eye but could be so deadly to its prey. Mesmerized by how it glided on the wind, Loren could think of nothing else.

A few minutes later, as the bird flew off into the distance to find a new place to hunt, Loren glanced around her yard. She could see her garden growing strong from the heat of the day and water she gave it. She appreciated the mountains in the far off distance and thought her and Sam needed to go for a hike in the near future. Then she looked towards the fire she had started to enjoy for the evening.

She watched as the flames danced within the wood. It turned from yellow to red and then to blue for just a moment. Then it would seem to disappear to have another flame take its place to have its chance to dance. Loren thought it seemed hypotonic and let it take her thoughts away.

Jessie stepped behind her and Loren was startled. "Oh. I didn't know you were home."

Jessie sat in a chair next to Loren and stared at the fire. It seemed to put her in the same trance Loren had been in moments before. She blinked her eyes to try and concentrate and looked away from the flames. "I just got home. Where's Sammie?"

"She was tuckered out from a long day of swimming . . . and looking through your closet," Loren giggled.

Jessie had a look of shock on her face. "You let her in my closet? Is there anything left?"

Loren laughed. "Yes. She put everything back where she found it. She is absolutely fascinated with your sense of style."

Jessie smiled. "Well . . . I do have pretty good taste."

"Ha-ha. I don't think I do that bad. Do I?"

"Umm . . ." Jessie glanced at Loren and smirked. "I'm just kidding. You have good taste too. I kind of thought we had the same style. That's why I found it weird Sam thinks I'm so intriguing. I guess it's just because I'm the aunt and not the mom. You're not supposed to be cool."

Loren looked away and let her attention focus on the flames again. She liked how they soothed her. It was like they carried all her worries away with the flames that extinguished behind the glowing kindling.

She heard Jessie groan beside her. Grinning, she looked towards her. "What's wrong with you?"

"Oh. I guess I'm trying to figure out what I did wrong in my life to have someone like Derik to mess it up."

Loren glanced at Jessie's arms and smiled. "Well, at least your arms are back to normal. Now the thought of what happened doesn't plague you every time you look down at them. I know it bothered me when I looked at your arms."

"Yeah. I know. I just don't know what to do from here. I'm kind of lost and I'm happy that you took me in to help get my head straight. You really are awesome . . . even though I dress better."

"You're so funny I forgot to laugh. But seriously, you're going to be fine. You're stronger than me. You've always been stronger than me. That's how I know that you'll figure it out and move on to a happy life. Who knows, you might meet mister right the next time you turn the corner."

Jessie stared at the flames and seemed to be a million miles away. When she spoke it sounded like she was half asleep. "I don't know. I don't think I'm gonna date any time soon. I think I'm on a man strike for now. I don't think it would be a good idea to get involved with anyone. I mean, how would I be able to trust him?" She paused for a moment but didn't take her eyes off the fire. "I think I'll just keep to myself."

Loren didn't know how to respond. She never thought she would get involved with another man either after she lost Craig. She hadn't been looking for a new companionship when she met Erik. It just kind of happened.

She admired Jessie's beauty and wondered how she didn't have a million men asking her out already. Although she knew that a lot of guys were intimidated by a beautiful woman and when you add owning your own successful business, it makes it even harder to approach her. Loren had seen countless guys look at Jessie, but when they heard of her business, they ran away. Loren guessed a beautiful, successful woman was too much to handle for some men.

Giggling to herself, Loren patted Jessie on the shoulder. "It will all work out. It always does. It may not end how we want it to end, but it ends how it should."

Jessie turned and stared at Loren. "Did you just hear yourself? You need to listen to what you're saying. Those words do apply to me but they apply to you too. You need to think about that. I mean, really Loren. You have a great guy in front of you and you can't move on with your life. I loved Craig too. I thought he was the best guy ever. He was great to you and was a wonderful dad. But, golly. You need to let him go. I know you think you hide it well but you don't. I see you struggling with the decision to let Erik into your heart." She looked away and stared into the darkness. She spoke softly and tenderly. "I love you Loren. I love Sam. And I want you both to be happy. You have to admit you're happy with Erik. Now . . . I'm tired and I'm going to bed. Love ya sissy." She didn't wait for a response and headed into the house.

Loren laughed to herself and pulled a blanket on top of her arms. She knew Jessie was right but it wasn't that easy. Everyone seemed to think she could change everything so quickly, but it wasn't that simple.

She heard a wolf howl in the distance and it gave her a chill. But being next to the fire gave her a sense of security and she relaxed. She let her eyes close and listened to the crackling of the fire and the soft breeze through the trees. She could smell the smoke from the wood and it somehow soothed her even more.

Her mind began to wonder and it stopped on Erik. She thought of the other day when they had been so close to running up stairs and shutting the door behind them. Loren almost regretted not letting the moment happen. She craved to have him close to her and make her feel loved and beautiful in an erotic way.

She imagined how his hands would have felt on her skin and the taste of his breath. She wondered how it would have been to have his body so close to her that it was hard to breathe. The thought made her moan to herself. She was tempted to call him and sneak to his house.

That would be okay wouldn't it? Jessie was here and she would make sure to be home before Sam woke up. Maybe she would. Maybe she could call him and say she wanted to pick up where they left off. She was sure he wouldn't have a problem with it.

But then, she began to think that Sam would get sick in the middle of the night and she wouldn't be there. Or, Sam would have a bad dream, like she sometimes did, and would go to crawl into bed with her and she'd be gone.

No. She wouldn't sneak off like a young girl. She would have to wait until they had the time together or until they were married and Erik moved into the house. But then, would it be different?

Would she be able to make love to him under the roof that she had built with another man?

With that thought, the image of Craig and her nestled in bed together popped into her mind. She wondered if she would be able to escape that image when Erik moved into their bedroom. Would she be able to take a bath with Erik or cuddle in front of the fireplace? She honestly didn't know.

It might be that Erik moved into the house and she wouldn't be able to be intimate at all. That wouldn't be fair to Erik. It wouldn't be fair to either of them.

They were able to kiss and laugh and hug, but would it go beyond that?

There were still so many unanswered questions and Loren didn't know how to answer any of them. She supposed they would just have to wait and see. If it didn't work with Erik in the house, then they would have to figure out a new plan. Or, maybe, she could remove the chains from around her heart so she could move on with her life.

That was one thing she didn't know if she could do. She didn't know if she could, or would, ever let Craig go. She didn't know how to even start. It had been three years. How long would it take? How long would she mourn his death? She didn't know if she ever wanted to stop mourning him. She had loved him with every breath of her body.

Maybe she felt like she had her chance at true love and that's all she deserves. Was that all she deserved?

Loren sat up and poked at the fire with a stick. She tried to forget her thoughts of Craig and Erik. It was like she had created a war within her mind that would never be won. Not when she was playing both sides. She needed to choose. She needed to choose if she wanted to be with Erik or live with the memory of Craig. But how was she to decide?

Stretching her back, Loren looked around the dark yard. She couldn't even see the shadows of the swing set or anything beyond it. Knowing it was time to head indoors, Loren grabbed some water and threw it towards the fire.

The sizzling sound of the extinguished flames made her feel instantly cold. It became even darker and she began to feel like she was the prey to a predator watching her in the dark. Grabbing her blanket, she found herself walking quickly to the door to go into the light of the house.

Loren turned to lock the door and thought she might see a wolf or bear rushing towards her. But she saw nothing but darkness and turned to go to her room.

Just as she put her night shirt over her head, she saw Sam at her door. Thankful she didn't call Erik to sneak to his house, Loren went to hug her daughter. "What's wrong? Why are you up?"

"I don't know. I guess I just wanted to snuggle tonight. Can I sleep with you?"

"Of course," Loren said. They crawled under the blankets and Sam cuddled close to her.

Loren breathed in the scent of Sam's freshly shampooed hair. Instantly, her thoughts of Craig and Erik disappeared. She was content with her sweet daughter sleeping beside her.

She knew these days would become less and less as Sam got older. So, for now, she would memorize every sweet scent and sound Sam made to tuck away.

Listening, Loren liked the soft rhythm of her breathing. She closed her eyes and thought about all the times she had with her daughter. All the times she had cuddled with her when she was tiny until now. It was wonderful to remember such good times.

Sam turned on to her side and exhaled.

Loren opened her eyes and watched as her daughter's chest rose and fell. She let the movement take her thoughts away and closed her eyes once again.

Chapter 11

*L*oren splashed water at Sam and she retaliated with a water gun and fired it at Loren's back. Loren turned, grabbed Sam, and threw her into the air. She splashed as she fell back into the water and water burst around the pool.

"Hey! I'm trying to get a suntan here. Quit splashing so much," Jessie hollered from the patio.

Loren and Sam grinned and they both grabbed a water gun. Aiming them at Jessie, they sprayed. They laughed as she jumped up and had a look of terror on her face.

"Dang it! I was nice and warm. Now I'm freezing!"

Sam rubbed her eyes like she was crying. "Oh, we're so sorry Aunt Jessie. Did we get your pretty swim suit all wet?" she whined.

Jessie glared at them. She walked towards the house, turned on the garden hose, grabbed the end and sprayed them with cold water.

Loren and Sam screamed when the ice cold water hit them. Sam dove under the water just to have Jessie squirt her again when she resurfaced. Loren grabbed a pool lounge chair and tried to deflect the water with it.

Jessie laughed and continued to spray them until she was bored. She shut the water off and put her hands on her hips. "Now, when I'm sunbathing, leave me alone," she said grouchily.

Loren and Sam stared at each other and burst into laughter. They grabbed their squirt guns and aimed them at Jessie again.

"Don't you dare! What's it take to get a little quiet around here?" Jessie yelled.

Loren stepped out of the pool and began to dry off. "Did you really expect that in this house? I mean, really Jess? What's wrong with you?"

"Nothing. I just wanted to sunbathe in peace. That's all," Jessie said and settled back down on the lounge chair.

"Well, we're sorry then." Loren turned her attention to Sam who was dumping water onto her own head from a bucket. "Sam let's head inside to change. We need to get ready to go to dinner anyways."

"Ah mom. I don't want to go out to dinner tonight. Do I have too? Can't I stay here with Aunt Jessie or go to Valerie's?" Sam moaned.

"No, Sam you can't. Erik asked for us both to go out. Not just me. Now get out and get into the shower young lady," Loren demanded.

Sam moaned and groaned and headed into the house. She looked back and pouted. "I thought you two were fighting? Why do I have to go?"

Loren gave Sam a serious look and pointed towards the house. "Now."

Jessie watched Sam go inside before she looked at Loren. "She can stay with me if she wants."

Loren shook her head. "No Jess. He asked for both of us. If we're going to try and work things out, then Sam needs to be part of the process. It's just not me that would be with him if we ever get married. Sam needs to put in an effort too."

Jessie flipped her hair over one shoulder and brushed through it with her fingers. "Okay. I'm just saying she could."

"Well, thanks for not saying that in front of her. That would've made it worse."

Jessie waved goodbye to Loren and closed her eyes. "Hey it's fine with me. I'll have some peace and quiet for a while."

Loren headed indoors to take a shower and heard Sam singing in the bathroom. She stood and listened. She loved to listen to Sam sing. As she listened, she thought it sounded angelic and sweet with her high pitched ten year old voice.

After a minute of enjoying the singing from behind the door, Loren headed towards her room to figure out what to wear. Finally, she choose some dark blue jeans with a button down silk shirt and heels. Satisfied with her choice, she picked out her lingerie and headed towards her bathroom.

When she stepped into the shower, she liked the hot water as it hit her skin and couldn't help but to let the water relax her. She liked the way the water pulsated against her and the thick steam surrounded her. She leaned against the side of the shower and let the water hit her shoulders to relieve some of the tension. Closing her eyes, she rolled her neck side to side a minute before she finally began to shampoo her hair. Reluctantly, she washed, shut off the water, and grabbed a towel.

Just as she got her underwear on, she heard Sam yelling behind the door. "Mom, I don't know what to wear. Do you think Aunt Jessie would let me wear something of hers?"

Loren continued to get dressed and hollered back. "I don't think so Sammie bear. I don't think you are quite big enough to fit into her clothes, do you?"

She heard Sam groan and storm off.

After dressing and drying her hair Loren went to check on her daughter. She found her sitting on her bed, in her robe, staring at her closet. "What's wrong?" Loren asked.

"I don't have anything to wear. We need to go shopping. All my clothes are for little girls. I'm not a little girl anymore. I mean look at it," she said pointing to the closet. "There's nothing there for a girl of my age."

Loren smirked and tried not to laugh. "Is this because you saw your aunt's closet?"

"Duh."

Again, Loren tried not to laugh. She went and sat on the bed with Sam and stared at the closet. "Well, I see a lot of nice things that don't look babyish. How about just wearing a pair of jeans and blouse like me?"

Sam glanced at what she was wearing and frowned. "No offensive mom, but I'm not dressing like you."

"Oh, I see. But if your aunt dressed like me it would look stylish."

"She's . . . different then you. She looks different, acts different, and even smells different."

"Well, I don't know what to tell you then. Why don't you ask Jess to help you find something?"

"Great idea. Thanks mom!" Sam said and raced for the backyard.

Moments later, Loren saw Jessie being dragged by the hand towards Sam's room. Jessie looked back at Loren and had her mouth open with a baffled look on her face. Loren giggled as she walked by Sam's room and went to sip on a glass of wine while she waited for her daughter to find the perfect outfit.

She heard Sam squeal with delight every so often and heard the closet door slam multiple times. The bathroom door opened and closed numerous times and finally, after a half hour, Sam came into the room.

"So what do you think mom?" Sam asked as she twirled around for her to see the entire outfit.

Loren raised her eyebrows and was astounded. Sam looked more grown up than she wanted. She was wearing tights with a long button down blouse, obviously Jessie's, and a silk scarf around her neck. She wore tall boots and her hair was tied back. She had on a small amount of makeup and looked beautiful. "Wow! I don't know what to say."

"I'm going to have Aunt Jessie help me with my outfits all the time!"

Jessie leaned against a wall and looked exhausted. "I don't know about that sweetheart."

Loren stood up and grabbed her purse. "Well, let's go you beautiful young woman."

Sam gleamed and headed out the front door.

Loren looked back at Jessie as she shut the door. "Thanks sis. She looks wonderful. Maybe a little too wonderful for my taste."

As they headed to the car, Sam couldn't stop talking about how they picked out her outfit. She was amazed how Jessie could put clothing together and make them look so good. She continued talking about the clothes and Jessie until they parked in front of the restaurant. Sam jumped out and was anxious to show her outfit to Erik and whoever else would look.

When they walked through the door, Erik was waiting. Loren gave him a small kiss and pointed towards Sam. "Sorry we're a little late. Someone had to look just right for the date. She doesn't want to dress like a *little girl* anymore."

"That's not good. We don't need a teenager yet."

Loren linked her arm in Erik's and liked how he spoke like they were already a family. She squeezed his hand and they went to take their seats. During the whole meal Loren would catch Sam glancing around to see if anyone was watching her. Loren would look at Erik and they would both smile.

After dinner, Sam talked them into taking a walk. She told them she wanted a little exercise after eating, but they both knew she wanted to show her outfit off just a little more. They agreed to take a walk with Sam leading the way. She walked a couple steps ahead of them as they strolled down the sidewalk. Loren held hands with Erik and enjoyed his company.

"Did you enjoy dinner?" Erik asked.

Loren tapped her stomach. "Maybe a little too much. I love pasta."

Erik put his arm around her shoulder and pulled her close. "I'm glad we're not fighting anymore. This is much better."

Loren leaned into him and felt his warmth. "Well, it was kind of a one sided fight."

"Yeah, I know. I jumped to conclusions. I understand now what's going on and that helps a bit."

"All you had to do was ask."

"I know Loren. I'm just anxious to get on with our lives. I want us to be together more than you'll ever know. Then when I saw Jessie there, I lost it. I'm sorry."

"It's just going to take time. That's all. I want to be with you too. I mean, I already feel like I am. It's just the complete adjustment I have to get used to."

"I promise I'll try to be more understanding and patient. But I need you to try a little harder to get past your feelings if you can?"

Loren moaned.

Sam stopped in her tracks and waited for them to catch up to her. "Can we go for ice cream?"

"Where do you put all that food?" Erik asked. "You ate as much as I did at the restaurant and I'm still full."

Sam shrugged her shoulders. "I don't know. I guess it's part of being a kid. I have a high motab . . . motaba . . ."

"Metabolism?" Loren asked.

"Yeah, that thing. Grown-up people don't have it. Why? Why don't you just go play like kids do? Then you would have a high motabo . . . whatever. You'd have it too."

Loren giggled. "I think you're wise for your age, Sammie bear. But I don't think you need any ice cream. You had plenty to eat." Loren watched Sam twirl in a circle and smiled. "Hey, didn't you have a desert at the restaurant missy?"

Sam looked at Loren sheepishly. "I guess so. But it wasn't very big."

Loren patted Sam on the shoulder. "I think you'll be alright without any ice cream."

Sam stomped her foot before she walked quickly to get a few steps ahead of them again.

Loren continued walking beside Erik and grinned. She thought it almost felt like a family being together like this. "So what do you want to do now?" she asked Erik, squeezing his hand in hers.

"I don't want to do anything but enjoy my time with you and Sam."

"I'm enjoying myself too. It's a beautiful night and I have wonderful company."

Erik kissed Loren on top of her head. "I really enjoyed the other day together too."

Loren glanced at Erik and blushed. She remembered how she had felt when they had been together a couple days earlier. "You do have an effect on me. That's for sure."

K A Neemeyer

Chapter 12

Life became easier over the next week and everyone seemed to get along. Jessie was completely moved in and feeling at home, Sam was happy to have both Valerie and Jessie to hang around during the day, and Loren was becoming comfortable with the idea of marriage.

It was a beautiful summer day and Loren opened the doors to "Good Mornings" to let the breeze blow in. She helped her customers and couldn't seem to stop smiling. And when Cody walked in, she was happy to see him too. "How's it going today?" she asked as he stepped up to the counter.

"Hey Loren. Just wanted to see if you had a break coming. I'm sure your boss would let you. Oh wait . . . you are the boss," he said amused by his own comment.

Loren looked around and saw that the rush of customers had finally slowed down. "Ha-ha. Yes, I have some time right now. Let me grab you a biscotti and coffee and me something too."

"How do you know if I want a biscotti?"

She raised her eyebrows and smiled. "Well, I can get you a cinnamon roll or scone or Danish if you prefer. Or some cheesecake or a croissant or muffin or cookie?"

"Okay, I'll take a biscotti. I was just joking. Do you make them here?"

"I wish I was that talented. No, I get them every morning from the bakery down the street. They like the free advertisement and me helping them with their sales."

Loren grabbed some finger food and coffee and brought them to the couch Cody seated himself at. She sat down and looked out the window to see people strolling up and down the street. "It's sure a nice day today. I can't wait to get out there."

"Why don't you go now? You're the boss."

"I have a job to do also. I'm shorthanded this morning anyways. The only reason I can sit down now is because it's slow in here at the moment."

"Well, I guess its good you're here. Or I'd be sitting by myself."

"That's right. Don't you ever work?"

"Yes. I had the afternoon off since I worked too many hours earlier this week. They don't like to pay overtime if they can help it. I'll go back in the morning."

"I see. So you decided to visit me? That's sweet."

"I thought maybe you would know some good shops for guys around here? I don't have much for summer clothes. I need help with a wardrobe."

"So you want shop names or me to help you?"

"You helping would be great. Think you could?"

"I think my sister would be better suited in that area, but I can give it a go."

"Your sister?"

"Yeah, my daughter seems to think my sister is the fashion queen and I'm boring and out of touch with style."

"Well, I'm just looking for some shorts and shirts. Not to step out on the red carpet. I think you'd help me just fine."

"Just shorts and shirts? Why do you need my help?"

"I'm color blind. A little help in that area is always good."

"Oh. I'm sorry."

"Why? You didn't make me that way. I was born with it. Not a big deal. It could be a lot worse."

"I can go with you in a couple hours if that's alright? I have to wait for Amber to get here."

"Sure. I can wait. But I don't want to take up too much room."

"You're fine. Just come up for a refill when you want. It's on the house." Loren smiled. "I know the boss," she said smiling.

A couple hours later, Loren and Cody wandered down the street towards Loren's favorite place to shop. She was comfortable walking next to Cody, like a brother or best friend. He was easy to talk to and made her laugh with his crazy sense of humor.

They wandered around the store and Loren helped Cody find multiple shirts and shorts. She had him try on every pair of shorts and every shirt to make sure they fit the same as how they looked on the hanger.

Cody would step through the dressing room door and would do a silly pose each time. He was comical and Loren had to wipe the tears from laughing so hard. After paying for his purchases, they headed down the street.

"What do you think Cody? You have enough or do you want more?"

"I think a couple more shirts and we can call it a day."

"I have to admit that this has been a blast. I haven't laughed this hard in a long time," Loren said.

"I've been having fun too. You're a pretty enjoyable lady to be around. Thanks for going with me. Who knows what I would have picked out? And with you helping me, I can remember what goes with what, so I match."

"I'm glad I could help."

"What's your last name?" Cody asked.

"Quinn? Why?" she answered, confused by the question.

"Just asking. Mine is Greene."

"Okay?" Loren put her hand out shake his. "Nice to meet you Cody Greene."

Cody shook her hand and walked towards the coffee shop. "Nice to meet you too, Loren Quinn. Want to have another cup of coffee?"

Loren got them each a cup of coffee and cinnamon roll. She sat down at the same couch they had been seated at before and looked at all his shopping bags and grinned. "All this shopping and I didn't buy one thing. My daughter would be upset if she knew that. Especially that I didn't buy her anything."

"She sounds interesting. Hopefully, someday I can meet her, and your sister."

"What about my boyfriend? You want to meet him too?"

Cody smirked. "Yeah, I'd like to meet him too. I don't know how he'd feel about you hanging around with me though."

Loren sat back and thought for a second. "I don't know. He gets moody sometimes and I don't know how he'll react. But he'll just have to see that we're just friends and there's no problem with it."

"I hope there's no problem. I like you and want to continue to be friends," Cody said and then took a big bite of his cinnamon roll.

"I like you too. I guess I should tell him about you so there's no surprises, huh?"

"Yeah, that might be a good idea," Cody agreed.

The next few minutes they sat quietly and nibbled on their cinnamon roll.

Loren thought about Erik and how he might react to having Cody as a friend. She knew he reacted badly to Jessie moving in and this was another man.

Maybe she should cut their time short and start avoiding Cody so he would get the hint that she didn't want to be around him. Maybe she should tell him right now that this is the last time they can do anything. Or maybe she should keep him as a friend. That's what he is, isn't he? He's just a friend.

She has other girlfriends so why can't she have a guy friend. Why should she feel uncomfortable with it? If Erik has a problem then it's his problem, not hers. She wouldn't have a problem if Erik had a friend who was a girl would she? Loren shook her head to herself and looked over at Cody. She watched him sip on his coffee and admired his features.

He definitely wasn't the kind of guy she would normally be attracted to. She didn't see him as a threat and Erik shouldn't either. Cody looked like the kind of guy a person would imagine grilling in their backyard with a funny apron on or out fishing with a wide brimmed hat, since she imagined he sunburned easily. No, he definitely didn't look like a threat. He was handsome, but not in a seductive way or a male model kind of way. He looked sweet and was sweet. He was funny and fun to be around.

Cody glanced at her. "What? Why are you staring at me?"

"I'm sorry. I was lost in thought."

"You do that a lot huh? What were you thinking about?"

"I was just thinking that this has been a nice day." She looked around and saw numerous customers walk through the door. "But the shops getting busy again and I should go to help out so . . ."

"I got the hint. I'll see you around then?" Cody asked with a smile.

"Definitely." Loren remained seated for a few more minutes after Cody walked out of the shop. She let the wonderful day get embedded in her mind and wished every day could be like this. Stress free and happy.

After closing up the shop, Loren headed home to see Erik's pick-up in the driveway. When she walked through the door she saw that he was seated on the couch, with Jessie.

He stood up and gave her a big hug. "Hello there love. I missed you today."

"Well, hello? I wasn't expecting to see you tonight. This is a nice surprise." She looked at them both suspiciously. They didn't seem to be fighting or have any kind of tension between them at all. She wondered when they began to get along again.

Jessie stood up, winked at Loren, and headed upstairs.

Loren sat down and motioned for Erik to sit with her. "What's up?"

Erik remained standing and grinned. "I was thinking." He knelt down on one knee in front of her, got a serious expression, and pulled a small box from his pocket.

Loren gasped.

"I was thinking that you said Sam wanted us to get married. I was thinking that I didn't want anyone else for the rest of my life. I was thinking that I Love you so much and want to show it to you and the world. I want everyone to know how I feel about you. I want everyone to see the love and know that you are off the market. Loren? Will you do me the honor of wearing this ring to show the world, and me, that we are in love and plan to marry?" He opened the box to display an engagement ring with numerous smaller diamonds surrounding a much larger princess cut diamond.

Loren sat back and felt a whirlwind of emotions. She stared at Erik, stared at the ring, and then stared back at Erik. "I don't know what to say."

Erik frowned. "What do you mean? You don't know what to say?"

"I wasn't expecting this. I . . . Yes! Yes, I will wear your ring and marry you!" Loren leapt from the couch and fell on top of Erik. She kissed him.

Laughter and clapping came from the kitchen. Loren sat up and saw Jessie and Sam. They were both smiling and Jessie had tears in her eyes. Sam looked genuinely happy and held her hands in the air as she continued to clap.

Loren looked back at Erik. "You surprised me. Why now?"

"Why now? Why not? And it's supposed to be a surprise." He sat up and pulled the ring from the box. He looked at her with love and placed the ring on her finger. "I love you Loren. I have loved you from the first day we bumped into each other. I love everything about you. Even your little quirks. I want to be part of your life, and Samantha's, forever and ever."

Loren looked down at her hand and admired the glistening diamond. She had tears streaming down her cheeks and was speechless.

"Well? Do you like it?" Erik asked.

Loren couldn't see the diamond from all the tears on her eyelashes. She wiped them away and held the ring up to the light so it would glisten even more. "I love it!"

Loren stood up to give Jessie and Sam hug and they all stared at the ring.

Sam hugged Loren again and looked up at her. "He even asked my permission. I told him, yes."

Loren held on to Sam and didn't know what to think or feel. She felt numb. She was overwhelmed. Sitting down, she didn't take her eyes off the ring. "I just . . . I don't know . . . I don't know how to feel. It's all so real now."

Sam sat beside her and gazed at the ring. "Wow. I hope I get a ring like this when I'm older. It's beautiful." She looked at Erik. "I really like it Erik. I really like the idea of you and mom getting married too. I mean it."

Jessie sat down on the other side of Loren and smiled. "It's about time. You guys should have been planning a wedding a long time ago. I think you two make a great couple."

Loren continued to stare at her ring. She couldn't put into words how she felt. It was exciting, yet scary. But as she stared at it, she thought it looked perfect on her hand. Although, it felt strange to have it around her finger. She looked up and saw

Erik grinning from ear to ear. "Thank you Erik. I love it. You did a good job picking it out."

Erik laughed. "I had a couple of helpers," he said and pointed towards Jessie and Sam.

Loren stood up and looked shocked. "You two were in on this? When did this all happen? When did you go shopping for it?"

Jessie lifted Loren's hand to look at the ring closer. "Oh, you know. We went a couple hours here and a couple hours there. We had to synchronize it while you were at work."

Loren shook her head. "I still can't believe it. You are all so wonderful to me. I have been blessed with each of you in my life. Thank you."

Jessie and Sam stood up and both gave Loren a hug at the same time. Erik joined in and gave them all a big squeeze until everyone was laughing.

Chapter 13

*I*t was strange to have a ring on again. Loren would fidget with it and turn it on her finger. She found herself staring at it all the time and still didn't know how to feel. She was torn between sweet happiness with Erik and trying to let go of Craig.

She had been wearing it for a week now, and it still didn't feel completely comfortable on her finger. She started to wonder if it ever would.

Loren pushed the thought aside and began to fold laundry. She couldn't believe how much there was with Jessie living with them now. It seemed to be even more of an endless chore.

Pushing her hair back from her face, Loren exhaled. She threw the laundry, from her lap, onto the couch and walked into her bedroom. Looking outside, she could see Sam playing on the swing set and felt a wave of love for her.

Sam was growing up so fast and to be able to watch her play on the swing set or play with her Barbie's began to be something rare to see. Loren noticed she was beginning to ask Jessie about make-up and searching through her closet for more *grown up* clothes to wear. She was worried about her hair and putting on jewelry. It all seemed to happen overnight.

Loren even caught her looking in her jewelry box for necklaces and bracelets to borrow. When Loren saw her reach for the heart necklace Craig given her, she got mad. She didn't mean to yell at Sam, but she had such an attachment to it and didn't need Sam losing it or breaking it. Sam had recoiled and ran from the room.

Loren looked towards her dresser, saw the necklace, and began to cry. She didn't know why she cried, but she didn't stop it either.

Grabbing the necklace, she fell onto her bed, and cried until there were no more tears. After she wiped her eyes, she held the necklace in the air and gazed at it. Once again, her heart ached for Craig.

She watched the necklace dangle in the air and it seemed to hypnotize her. She stared at it until her eyes grew heavy and finally closed.

When she woke, she looked at the clock and saw she'd slept for almost an hour. She was surprised that Sam hadn't waken her. Instantly, she got a bad feeling.

Loren wrapped the necklace around her hand and ran into the living room. She began to call Sam's name. She called for her casually at first but when she didn't get an immediate response, she grew worried. After a minute of hollering for her, and not getting an answer, Loren's voice got louder and louder to the point she was yelling. There still was no answer. Loren felt sick to her stomach. She rushed to the back door and looked towards the swing set. Sam wasn't there.

Loren ran to the edge of the patio and yelled Sam's name. She yelled it a dozen times before she ran back into the house and began to yell it more. She ran to every room and Sam was in none of them.

Loren felt perspiration under her shirt. Bad thoughts plagued her mind and her heart was pumping fast. She was frantic.

She began to think about what if a bear came close to their house or some other wild animal? What if someone was driving by and saw her out by herself? What if she had gotten hurt and had hollered for Loren, but she didn't hear her?

Loren shook her head and tried to push the thought away. She needed to remain calm to think straight. She needed to remember where she had looked and where to look next. Loren shook her head again and cursed at herself for falling asleep.

Trying to think, she started to check any place she hadn't been to yet. Racing to the backyard again, she headed to the tree house. Frantically, she climbed the ladder and prayed Sam would be sitting inside. Loren pushed the door open. "Sam!"

The tree house was empty. All except for a couple Barbie dolls and a box of paper and markers.

Loren began to feel like she was going to vomit. Her legs began to shake with every step back down the ladder. Her mouth was dry. Her hands were trembling.

Quickly, Loren ran to the swing set and began to look for any indication of Sam. Or an animal. When she saw no indication of an animal she breathed a sigh of relief. Then she began to head towards the house and scanned the yard as she walked.

When she entered the house, she yelled for Sam many more times. She tried to take a deep breath to calm her nerves and think clearly. She snapped her fingers with a new idea and ran for the phone. She called Jessie. "I can't find Sam!"

Jessie gave the bouquet of flowers to her customer and walked towards the backroom of her flower shop. "What do you mean, you can't find her?"

"I fell asleep. I slept for almost an hour and when I woke up . . . I can't find her Jessie! What do I do?! Oh my God! What did I do? Why did I fall asleep?"

"Okay. First you have to try and calm down. Did you look in her room and the tree house?"

"Yes and yes. I looked everywhere. I yelled and yelled. I can't find my little girl!"

Jessie had a concerned and serious voice when she spoke. "I'm going to hang up Loren. I'm coming home and I'll call Erik. I'll be there in a few minutes. Can you hold on? I'll call you on my cell after I call Erik. Hold on. We're coming."

With Jessie's last word, she heard the phone go silent. She slid to the floor and began to cry. Then she shook her head and was determined to convince herself that nothing was wrong. She knew Sam was hiding from her or just didn't hear her because she had on head phones or something.

Determined, Loren began to search the house again. She went into every room. She looked under every bed and in every closet. She looked in the bathrooms and bath tubs. She checked the laundry room and storage room. Sam was nowhere.

Loren heard her cell phone ring from the kitchen and sprinted to get it. It was Jessie.

Loren was frantic. "What do I do? Are you almost here?"

"I'll be there in a few minutes. Erik is on his way too."

"Should I call the police yet? How long does a mother have to wait when their child is missing?"

"Let Erik and I help you first. Then we'll call if we can't find her. But I'm sure we will. Don't worry Loren. We will. I see the driveway. I'm going to hang up."

Loren rushed to the front door and saw Jessie driving fast up the drive.

Jessie slammed on the brakes and dust flew around the car. She ran through it as she rushed to Loren and hugged her tight. She had a worried look and took Loren by the hands. "Okay, where haven't you looked?"

"I think I've looked everywhere."

"Okay Loren. There is no *I think*. You have to know. Did you look everywhere in the house?"

"Yes! Yes! Yes! I've looked everywhere in the house. I even looked in the dryer. She's not in the house!"

"Loren getting mad at me won't help find her. Let's go back into the backyard." Jessie almost dragged Loren with her large steps and fast pace.

They stepped out onto the patio and Jessie yelled Sam's name. Loren joined her and then heard a wolf howl in the distance. Just hearing his call made her cringe with fear.

"Sam! Sam! Where are you?" Jessie yelled. She turned and saw Loren getting pale. "Loren sit down. I don't need you falling over on me or passing out. Get control sis! We'll find her."

"Did you find her?" Erik yelled as he ran around the corner of the house and into the backyard.

"No. Not yet," Jessie said.

Erik kneeled beside Loren. "We'll find her. What does she like to do during the day when your home?"

Loren felt dizzy. "I don't know."

Erik frowned. "You don't know? What's that mean?"

Loren was on the verge of tears. "She's growing up too fast. She's different from even a month ago. She isn't my little girl anymore. I don't know what she does. She's . . ."

"Okay, okay. Let's start looking," Erik said. Then he took Loren's hand to help her to her feet.

Loren had a queasy feeling. She began to feel like she had when she got the phone call about Craig. "Oh Sam! Don't leave me! Don't leave me like your dad did!"

Erik closed his eyes for a moment. "Loren, she's going to be fine. She didn't leave you. You stay here. Jessie and I will look for her."

Loren looked into Erik's eyes. "No! I'm fine. Let's go," Loren said and headed out towards the field behind the yard.

The three of them hollered and hollered Sam's name. They began to walk out further from the house where Sam should never go on her own. Then they half walked and half ran up a tall hill. When they reached the top and looked down, they saw her.

"Sam!" Loren cried.

Sam looked up and held a bouquet of wild flowers in her hand. She smiled at them and held the flowers in the air. "Look what I found. All by myself."

Loren ran down the hill and hugged her daughter. She held her back for a moment and looked her over. "You're okay? You're not hurt?"

Sam cocked her head to side and stared at Loren. "What's wrong?"

"You! That's what's wrong. Didn't you hear me calling for you? I've been looking for you forever. I thought that . . ."

"Mom. I'm fine. See," she said and held out the flowers. "I wanted to surprise you. I went to your room and saw you sleeping. I saw you were holding the necklace daddy gave you and knew you were feeling bad for him being gone. So I thought I'd get you some flowers to cheer you up."

Loren fell to her knees. She looked down at her hands and noticed she was still holding the necklace. She had been holding it so tightly that an outline of the chain and heart was indented into her hand. She put the chain into her other hand and rubbed the indentation with her fingers. She wondered if Craig had been with her in spirit to find Sam and she began to cry.

Jessie rubbed Loren's shoulder for a moment, and then she hugged Sam. "You scared us horribly. We were yelling for you. We thought you were lost or hurt. Didn't you hear us?"

Sam's arms fell to her side and she looked confused. "I thought I heard mom earlier, but the wind was blowing so I thought it was nothing. Then I heard you a second ago, but I wanted to get one last flower. I didn't think it was a big deal."

"You can't wander from the house this far away. Especially without an adult," Erik said sympathetically.

"Oh. I didn't mean to scare you mommy. I just wanted to do something nice." Sam gave Loren a hug and put her head on top of Loren's. "I'm sorry."

Loren stood up and stared at Sam with tears on her eyelashes. "I appreciate the gesture, but you're grounded."

Chapter 14

*L*oren turned on her windshield wipers and couldn't believe how fast the storm had formed. It had gone from sunny skies to dark in about an hour and the heavy rains which followed were making it hard for her see through her windows.

This was odd summer weather for Montana. They usually got dry thunderstorms or a little light rain every now and again, but never storms like this. She hadn't even brought an umbrella since rain usually didn't come with the thunder. Concentrating, she took the car off of cruise control so she could pay close attention to any animals that were crossing the road.

She was already frazzled from the last couple days of Sam whining about being grounded and not understanding why she couldn't leave the back yard. Sam thought she was big enough to take care of herself and Loren began to feel scared. She wasn't ready for such attitudes and hoped it was just a phase Sam was going through.

Loren tried to think back when she was younger and how she'd acted at that age. She could remember bits and pieces, but she couldn't remember if she wanted to grow up that fast. She wished she could make Sam understand that it was hard to be a grown up sometimes and that being a kid, for as long as she could, was the best thing ever.

Switching on the defog button, Loren leaned closer to the steering wheel to see the road more clearly. The storm became even more intense and she wondered if it was such a good idea to head in to town. But she knew that they needed more milk and other groceries and she had no idea when the storm would end.

Through the pounding of the rain, she heard her cell phone began to ring. Not thinking she could concentrate on two tasks at one time with such heavy rain, Loren pulled over to the side of road. When she saw it was "Good Mornings" calling, she rolled her eyes and wondered if it was such a good idea to run her own business.

It seemed that more and more problems arose that no one but her could take care of. Even with all the training she had given her employees, there were still a lot of areas she needed to concentrate on training more. Trying to make a mental note, Loren decided to have an employee meeting so she wouldn't have to be at the shop every day, and what seemed, every hour.

Turning left, instead of turning right to go to the grocery store, Loren parked and ran into the shop with her hands over her head. She was drenched by time she got inside and cursed under her breath. Grabbing a towel from behind the counter, she dried herself as much as she could. Then she tried to fix the steam wand, confused why it kept clogging.

When she finally fixed the contraption, she glanced around the shop and saw Cody sitting at a table. He was looking down at his cup of coffee and was tapping his foot under the table. He looked troubled.

She stepped from behind the counter, twirled her engagement ring around her finger, and went to say hello. "What's up Cody? Why are you out in this weather?"

Cody looked up and seemed surprised to see her. "Hey, I didn't know if you would come in today. I had a question for you."

Loren sat down and put her hands in her lap. "Okay? What?"

He swished the coffee in its cup and suddenly looked nervous. "You said you have a sister right?"

"Yeah. Why?"

Watching the coffee move in cup, he spoke quietly. "Well . . . there's a thing I have to go to and I thought it might be good to bring a date?"

Loren smirked. "A date? How do you know that she's available?"

Cody moved around in his chair. "I didn't. I was just hoping." He looked up at Loren with an apprehensive look on his face. "Is she? Available?"

"She just came out of a bad relationship. I don't know if she's up for dating."

"No, not dating. Just one date. That's all," Cody said.

Loren looked at him seriously. "And there's no one else to ask? You don't know her. You are really desperate huh?"

"I suppose. I guess I figured she would look like you and you're not too bad."

Loren tilted her head to one side. "Actually, you have seen her. She was with me at the bar the night you screamed at me." Loren giggled then got a puzzled look on her face. "Not too bad? Is that supposed to be a compliment?"

Cody leaned forward and stared into her eyes. "Yes. That's a compliment." He smiled and then his smiled faded when he looked over Loren's shoulder. "There's a guy staring at me and it doesn't look like he likes me sitting with you."

Loren glanced back to see Erik standing in the doorway. He had a look on his face combined with anger and confusion. Along with being drenched from the rain, he looked more angry than confused.

Erik stepped behind her and squeezed her shoulder. "Who's this Loren?"

Loren felt herself jump with the pressure of Erik's grasp. It was like she'd been caught with her hand in the cookie jar. She knew she had done nothing wrong, but she hadn't told Erik about Cody and knew she was guilty of that. "Hey, Erik. This is my friend Cody. He stopped by to see if Jessie would be available for a date."

Erik continued standing behind Loren. "Hmm. He knows about Jessie, but I don't know about him? What's going on?"

Loren was uncomfortable with Erik towering over her. She couldn't see his face and when she looked at Cody, she knew Erik wasn't smiling. She turned her body in her chair so she could look up at him. "Why don't you sit down?"

"I don't feel like sitting down. What's going on here I asked?" Erik said sternly.

Loren shook her head and was getting irritated with how Erik was responding to her speaking to another man. She was a grown woman and knew how to make good choices. She didn't need a jealous fiancé.

What if Cody was a man from a company coming to speak to her pertaining to the coffee shop? What if it was any kind of a business deal and he walked into the shop? "Erik, he is a friend. There is nothing *going* on. Like I said, he stopped by to see if Jess might go on a date with him."

Cody shifted in his seat and then stood up. "Hi. I really only came in here to ask about her sister. We really are just friends."

Erik snorted. "Just friends? Why haven't I heard about you then?"
Loren stood up. "Erik, stop it. It's my fault for not telling you that I have a guy as a friend. We drink coffee, shop, and talk about stuff."

Erik grabbed Loren's left hand and put it in front of Cody. "Have you seen this?"

Cody stared at Loren's ring. "No. Honestly, I hadn't seen the ring, but that doesn't have anything to do with us. I don't need to put a ring on her finger to be her friend. I'm new in town and Loren has been very helpful helping me with stuff."

"Stuff? What kind of stuff?" Erik said accusingly.

Loren looked at Erik and saw him sizing up Cody. She didn't need a fight in her shop or anywhere else. "Knock it off Erik. I just told you what *stuff* we do. It's a totally innocent friendship. I have a friend who is a guy. No big deal."

Erik made is hands into fists. He glared at Loren. "No big deal? No big deal? Really Loren? You have another man in your life and you think it's no big deal? Put yourself in my shoes. What if you walked into my office and I had another woman laughing and being a little too close to me?"

Loren took a deep breath. "Well, if I saw it from your point of view, I guess I would be reacting the same. I'm sorry for not telling you, but Cody and I are only friends. I promise. I'm not going to go through everything I have with you and throw it away. I'm not going to be having an affair in my shop where the entire town could see. I'm not the kind of woman to have an affair at all." Loren took another deep breath and tried to get control of her emotions. She glanced around the shop before looking back at Erik and speaking quietly. "I love you and only you. I'm not going to put myself, or Sam, into a bad situation. Now, can you please sit down and stop making a scene?"

Erik shook his head. "I don't know about this anymore. First your sister moves in with you and now this. I give you a ring and you're sitting with another man."

Loren grabbed Erik's arm. "Knock it off. Please sit down. This is ridiculous."

Erik reluctantly sat down at the table. "Fine. I'll hear you out."

Loren and Cody glanced at each other before they also sat down.

Cody pulled his chair closer to the table. "Look. I know this probably looks bad to you. I have been cheated on in the past and I know the emotions you're feeling. I really do. But I promise there is nothing going on other than some friendly talk. I didn't know about the engagement, but I do want to say congratulations."

Erik stared at Cody as he spoke and his demeanor seemed to relax a little. "I guess I might have reacted a little fast. I admit that." He looked at Loren and tried to smile. "I'm sorry Loren. That's twice I jumped the gun on your actions. It just didn't look good when I walked in the door."

Loren squeezed Erik's arm. "I'm not going to do anything to jeopardize our relationship. I promise. I've already put you through enough and don't plan on making things harder."

Erik sighed. "Alright." He glanced at Cody and put his hand out to shake. "Sorry Cody. I guess I was a little defensive of my future bride."

Cody shook Erik's hand and relaxed. "I don't know what to say. Not to put it on Loren, but I assumed she said something about us hanging out."

Loren grinned. "You just sold me out Cody. See if I ever give you free coffee again."

All three laughed and the tension disappeared. Loren left them alone for a moment to grab herself and Erik some coffee and came back to them both smiling. "What's so amusing?"

Erik took his coffee from her and laughed. "We were just saying how you must be a pretty wonderful woman to get so uptight about."

Loren blushed.

Erik grabbed her hand and squeezed it. "I am sorry for overreacting. Especially in your shop."

Loren smiled. "Hey, like I said, I'm not going to jeopardize what we have. Cody is more like . . . a brother or a best friend I've known for years. We mesh well together." She looked at Cody and smirked. "Although when we first met it didn't seem like it."

Cody laughed. "Yeah. I was kind of an ass that night."

Erik sat back in his chair and stared at them. "Anyone going to fill me in on the story or do I have to draw conclusions again."

Loren squeezed his hand. "Well . . . if you would have met him like I did . . . you might have put a fist in his face."

"Really?" Erik asked.

Cody shifted in his chair and looked nervous. "I wasn't very nice the first night we met each other . . . or the second or third. But I finally figured out that you have a pretty awesome lady here and we've been good friends ever since."

Chapter 15

"Can I be ungrounded now?" Sam asked as she dried the dishes from the sink.

Loren looked out the window and saw it raining just as heavily as it had the day before. "What would you do if I did unground you? It's raining cats and dogs out there," she said and pointed out the window.

Sam rolled her eyes. "I want the option to leave or do what I want."

"The option? You have to remember you are only ten young lady. You're not sixteen or eighteen."

Sam threw the towel on the counter and put her hands on her hips. "Well, if this is how it's going to be then I can't wait to move out!" she screamed and ran towards her room.

Loren heard Sam's door slam shut. She leaned on the counter and stared out the window at the rain. She breathed a big sigh and continued to put dishes away. She got lost in her thoughts.

Maybe it wasn't a good idea for Jessie to move in. It seemed Sam's attitude began about the same time Jessie had taken the spare room, but Loren tried not to blame her. She hoped it was the age or the stress of the marriage ideas.

Loren didn't know what to do. There seemed to be too much going on for her to handle anymore. She needed a break.

Plopping down on the couch, Loren stared at her ring. Then she glanced up at the fire place and her thoughts went to Craig.

She could remember the first time they had started a fire when the house was new. It had been a rainy day like this one and Craig was soaked by time he came into the house with the fire wood. It took five minutes to get the fire started and Craig stood close to try and get warm.

Loren remembered staring at him and seeing the form of his abs, beneath the wet shirt. She had an instant desire for him. She walked behind him and pulled his shirt over his head and ran her hands across his chest and stomach before he turned and kissed her. She remembered her legs had gotten weak from the passion of his kiss before they fell to the floor. Loren had tugged at the rest of his wet clothes until they were in a pile on the floor. Then she grabbed a blanket off the couch and covered them both.

While under the covers, they began to feel one another and the heat began to intensify between them. Loren had looked into his eyes and saw a hunger she knew she would be pleased to satisfy.

Slowly, Craig had removed her clothes and began to caress her soft skin. His touch made her feel like she was going mad. She wanted him to stop, but she wanted him to continue until she couldn't take anymore. She wanted it to last for as long as possible.

Finally, they gave into the sensations and had made love for what seemed eternity. They touched, caressed, nibbled, and tasted until they were both out of breath. When they were both satisfied, they had fallen asleep, in front of the fire, intertwined together.

Loren closed her eyes and imagined Craig sitting in front of the fire with his skin glistening from the sweat and rain. She could see his eyes sparkling and him telling her that he loved her forever and a day. She could almost smell his cologne and found herself leaning towards the fireplace to try and catch a scent of him.

She missed him. She missed him more than anything in the world. He had become her world, and when he died, her world never became the same again.

Wrapping her arms around herself, Loren stared at the cold fireplace. She admired the ledge stone surrounding it. She liked the earth tone colors and was very content with the decision to have it throughout the house. It was around the fireplace, in the kitchen, and even around the tub in Loren's bathroom.

When they first had made their decisions on the counter tops and other décor, which Loren saw it in a brochure and fell in love. She told Craig but he wasn't as excited about it as her. Nonetheless, she was able to persuade him with kisses and begging. She remembered when it was first applied to the walls that and she jumped for joy from all the beauty and that Craig had said he liked it too.

Loren liked that she had so many good memories. She liked reminiscing about her life with Craig and enjoyed the feeling it gave her when she thought of their happy times. She had been truly happy and wished he was still with her.

Feeling the ring on her finger, Loren thought of Erik and how he made her happy too. Maybe if they got all new furniture she would be able to have a fresh start with him. Or maybe they did need to look for a new house so she wouldn't have thoughts of Craig so often.

No. She didn't want to take Sam away from her home. The house was built sturdy and she and Craig planned on living there until they went to a retirement community. They had laughed about Sam putting them into a home and her taking over the house. Although, they also thought they would have more children. They discussed having three or four by time they were forty.

But now, Loren only had Sam and didn't plan on having any more kids. She knew Erik would probably bring the issue up, but she was positive that she didn't want to get pregnant again. Partially because she had such a hard pregnancy with Sam and partially because she only wanted to have Craig's children. Maybe that was selfish, but, right now, that was how she felt and didn't see it changing.

Loren put her hands on her stomach. She worked so hard to get it flat again and couldn't imagine going through the process a second time. It wasn't the wonderful pregnancy that so many other woman enjoyed. When she was pregnant with Sam, she had gained forty pounds. She was so scared that she would miscarry, or that the baby wasn't getting enough nutrients, that she had eaten too much. Then she had horrible morning sickness that went from the morning until the night for six months. She was miserable during the whole pregnancy and was ecstatic when she felt her first contraction. Loren was happy to give birth to her little girl and be done with pregnancy.

Loren heard the front door open and saw Jessie hiding beneath a magazine, trying to escape the rain. Her clothing was drenched and she looked tired.

Jessie said, "This day was horrid. People trampled in mud and rain all day. It was like I was cleaning up after a hurricane by time I locked the doors. There was a mat in front of the door, but no one could wipe their shoes on it. Nope. They had to make a huge mess."

Loren figured it was the same way at the coffee shop and was happy she didn't have to deal with it today. "Sorry Jess. Want me to start the fireplace up for you?"

Jessie wrinkled her forehead and tilted her head to one side. "What? No. It's summer time Loren. I'm gonna take a hot shower and grab some warm clothes for a while. I feel cold down to my bones," Jessie said and headed up the stairs. "I'm using your shower by the way."

Loren ran her fingers through her hair and walked into the kitchen to make some hot tea. It was summer, but she felt cold like it was the middle of December. She figured it was from the cloudy skies and rainy day.

Holding on to the hot cup to let the heat penetrate her skin, Loren sat back on the couch and stared out the window. The rain was still coming down in sheets and she hoped her garden wasn't washed away with all of the moisture. She was baffled with so much precipitation this time of year. Usually she was out watering her garden every morning and sometimes in the evening too.

A while later, Jessie came back down the steps wearing flannel pajamas and a winter robe. She had on a stocking hat and her hands were in the pockets of the robe.

Loren giggled when she saw her. "I guess you were cold. Got enough clothes on?"

"Hey, I need to warm my bones," Jessie said as she sat on the couch next to Loren and cuddled up next to her.

"You're making me sweat," Loren remarked and tried to push Jessie away.

"Ah, come on. I'm freezing."

Loren grabbed a blanket and threw it at her. "Here, take this and get off me," she giggled. She watched as Jessie tucked the blanket around her until it looked like she was in a cocoon. Remembering Cody, Loren tried to figure out the right words to say to ask Jessie to go out with him. "I need to ask you something. First I need to tell you something. Did I ever tell you that I have a male friend?"

Jessie sat up. "No. When did this happen?"

"Remember that guy from the bar that was screaming in my face?"

"Yeah. He was a jerk. Why?"

"Well, he had come into the shop a couple times and tried to start a fight with me there."

Jessie sat up straight and stared at Loren. "Why didn't you tell me? I would have kicked his butt."

Loren chuckled to herself and knew that Jessie would have. "All that stuff was going on with Derik and you were the priority at that time. Anyways, he came in to yell at me and we had a little conversation. I explained that I'm not generally like that and he apologized for being like he was. It was rather sweet."

Jessie's mouth opened and no words came out.

"What?" Loren asked.

"You let it go that easy? After he called you a dog and said such horrible things? What's wrong with you?"

"Jessie, it's nothing. He apologized. I apologized. Now its water under the bridge." Loren took a sip of her tea and watched her sister's expression. "Really. He's a nice guy. We've even gone shopping and had coffee together a couple times."

"Hmm." Jessie put her head back on the couch for a moment before she sat up and stared at Loren again. "What about Erik? You know how he was with me moving in here. Have you told him? This may not be a good thing Loren. I mean, it's another guy."

Loren stared at her cup. "Yeah. He came into the shop yesterday while Cody and I were talking."

"Cody?"

Sarcastically Loren said, "Yes Jessie. Cody. That's his name." She put a pillow behind her head and tried to get comfortable. "Anyways, Erik came in and it didn't go to good at first. He started being defensive but finally calmed down and we all talked for quite a while. It was kind of nice."

Jessie blinked her eyes numerous times. "Erik didn't rip the guy's head off? Loren you get yourself into these situations and come out smelling like a rose. How do you do it? I can only imagine how Derik would've been if *I* would have a male friend."

"Well, the point is, is that Cody is really sweet. He's new in town and doesn't know too many people. Now to the question." Loren hesitated. "Would you be willing to go on a date with him for a work thing?"

Jessie stood up and the blanket fell to the floor. She pointed at Loren, put her hands to her sides, pointed at Loren, and then stared at her. "You're trying to set me up? And with a guy who talked to you so horribly? You want *me* to go out with him? What's wrong with you? Don't you remember what just happened to me? Don't you care about what I just went through? Derik is out of my life but . . . What's wrong with you?"

Loren didn't know how to respond. She knew Jessie would react, but not like this.

Jessie picked up the blanket, wrapped it around her shoulders, and fell back onto the couch. She pulled the blanket around her and sighed. "When did he ask?"

"Yesterday."

"Why didn't you ask me last night?"

"Would've you responded better?" Loren asked.

Jessie scowled. "No."

Loren tried not to laugh. "Then what's the difference?"

Jessie cuddled further under the blankets. "I don't understand you Loren. You're too forgiving and easy going. What kind of *thing* did he want to take me too?"

"I don't know. I didn't ask."

"Okay. When did he want to go out?" Jessie asked.

"I don't know."

"Really Loren? What do you know?"

"I guess I could call him. I have his number somewhere." Loren tilted her head and smiled. "So you are willing to go out with him?"

Jessie looked like she was in deep thought. She didn't speak for at least a minute. "I don't know. I did think he was a little cute." She put her hand to her mouth. Her words came out muffled. "Maybe a night out would be good."

Loren gasped. "Really? Sweet. I'll call him and see when and where. Maybe we can all get together so it's not so awkward."

K A Neemeyer

Chapter 16

*T*he sun was shining, the grill was hot, and a soft breeze was blowing. Everyone seemed to be happy and Loren watched as Sam splashed in the pool. She looked up at the sky to see streaks of clouds which didn't seem to move at all. Looking out towards her garden, she smiled as she saw the greenness of the plants and ripening eggplant on the vines. Looking back towards the house, she heard Jessie and Cody involved in a political discussion and Erik smiling as he listened in.

Loren went inside to prepare the burgers and steak to throw on the grill. She checked the pie in the oven and the potatoes on the stove. Washing some fruit, she began to cut it for a salad and she was pleased that the day was going so well.

Erik walked behind her and hugged her waist. "Seems like Jess and Cody are getting along pretty good. Hopefully they don't disagree too much. With

Jessie's short temper and what you told me about Cody, it could get pretty ugly."

Loren glanced out to the table they were sitting at and saw Cody scoot his chair closer to Jessie. "I think they are getting along splendidly. I wasn't for sure how it would go, but they hit it off right when they introduced themselves."

"I have to say that it's good to see Jessie happy again. I can't remember the last time I saw her smile so much. Even when she was with Derik. Things must have been worse between them then any of us ever thought," Erik said.

Loren turned in Erik's arms and hugged him. "She told me some wild stuff. Derik was something, that's for sure. Remind me to tell you more about it later. Want to help me get the fruit salad and asparagus ready?"

Erik grabbed a knife and trimmed the woody ends off the asparagus and then began to chop some apples.

He whistled while he worked and Loren shook her head and grinned at him.

Loren said, "Erik I really am in love with you. Its times like right now that I fall in love with you more."

Erik smiled sweetly. "Why? Because I know how to whistle?"

Loren laughed. "No. It's because you have such a good personality and are so willing to help me out to make me happy. You're a good man."

"Why thank you Loren. That means a lot. I'll try to remember this moment when you're mad at me for something else."

Loren splashed water from her hand at him. "Ha-ha. We don't have that many disagreements." She smiled. "If you do what I say there's never a problem."

Erik snickered. "Maybe you need to listen to what I say. Then we would be already married and I could cuddle with you every night and wake up to you every day. We could cook together all the time and I could come home to you instead of an empty house."

Loren put her hands on her hips. "You don't go home to an empty house. You have Sheena, the little stray you took in a while ago."

"You know what I mean Loren. She's gonna be your dog too. Just look at her laying down so nice on the patio. She's a good dog. Very gentle. I'm glad I found her, or her finding me. Whichever. But at least I have something to go home to for right now."

Loren looked out to see the dog laying at Jessie's feet. Every few minutes Jessie would bend down to pet Sheena's head and Sheena would lick her hand. She was a multicolored mutt with black, gray, and brown mixed in with a white coat. She looked like she might be a mix between an Australian Shepard and a Blue Tick Heeler. She was a little over a year old and was a sweet dog. The only problem Loren had was she wasn't a fan of dog hair on the furniture and knew Sheena already was in the habit of laying on Erik's couch. Shrugging her shoulders, she figured she would just have to get a dog blanket and train Sheena to only lay on it.

After finishing the fruit salad, Loren and Erik carried out the food to put on the grill. Loren lifted the lid and the smell of hot briquettes made her mouth salivate for the food that still had to cook. She placed the meat and asparagus on the cooking grid and closed the lid. She wandered to the pool and watched Sam dive under the water to find water sticks she had thrown in. When Sam came above the water she wiped her eyes and looked at Loren.

Loren grinned at her. "How's the water?"

"It's perfect. Going to come in with me mom?"

Loren put her hands in the water and liked the temperature of it. "Maybe after we eat. Right now I have to cook. Did you want a steak or burger for dinner?"

"A burger's fine. Hey mom?"

"Yes Sammie bear."

"I'm sorry for talking to you like I did the other day. I shouldn't have done that. You're a good mom."

Loren had tears well up in her eyes and she pushed them back. "Thank you Sammie. That means a lot to me."

"I'm really sorry mom. I just . . . I didn't like being grounded. And I only went to get the flowers for you to make you smile."

"I know that. It was just that you wandered off so far. There are so many animals out here Sammie. They're not tame. They'll hurt you if they need to feed their babies or feel threatened by you," Loren said with a serious tone.

Sam leaned on the edge of the pool. "I know that. I guess I was just thinking about making you smile and not the other stuff." She glanced at Sheena. "Maybe if we had a dog I could wander a little further because the dog would protect me."

Loren saw Sam staring at Sheena and smiled. "She will live with us when Erik and I ever get married. You'll have to wait until then."

"We can have *two* dogs. One now and another one when Sheena comes here."

Loren splashed water at Sam's face. "Don't push it young lady. I had a dog when I was younger and it was really hard when she died. I guess I'm scared to have another one and go through the pain again."

"Ah mom. They say there's a hundred percent chance that everyone and everything will die you know."

She waved back at Sam as she walked away. "I know that smarty pants."

Loren went back to tend to the grill and Cody took the spatula from her hand. "I'll take care of this. You take a load off."

Loren grinned at him and went to sit with Jessie and Erik. She grabbed her ice tea and twirled it in the glass. She took a big swallow and glanced back at Cody. He was just as she had imagined except for no apron on. His red hair gleamed in the sun light and he had a serious expression as he flipped the burgers and steaks. Glancing back at Jessie, Loren saw she was watching Cody too. "So what do you think sis? He's a pretty good guy, don't you think?"

Jessie pulled her hair into a pony tail and put a band around it. "He's alright. I guess I have to give you credit when you said he's nice. He is quite the gentleman."

Erik chimed in, "I have to admit that I think he's a pretty good guy too." He looked over at Jessie. "Is he really your type? I guess I don't see you with a guy like him."

Jessie looked at Erik confused. "My type? What's my type Erik?"

Erik raised his hands defensively. "I didn't mean anything bad by it. It's just he's totally different than Derik."

Jessie nodded her head. "Yes he is. That's the point. Maybe if I go totally opposite than what I think I like, I'll find a keeper. Not saying that Cody and I are dating or anything."

Loren saw Cody glance back at Jessie and knew that he could hear the conversation. "What do you think Cody?"

Jessie looked startled and embarrassed that Cody had heard her. "Sorry Cody. I didn't mean it in a bad way."

Cody twirled the spatula in his hand. "No offense taken. I just want to know if you'll go to the dinner thing for work. Will you?"

Jessie blushed. "I guess I could. But I need to know what day and time. Kind of helps to get ready that way," she said sarcastically.

Cody smiled. "It's tonight. In about three hours."

Jessie jumped out of her seat. She looked frantic and looked down at her nails. "Tonight? I can't do it tonight. I have to do my nails and I don't have anything to wear. I don't even know what to wear. Really? Tonight?"

Cody started laughing. "No. It's not until next week. I just like to mess with people."

Jessie grabbed her glass of ice water and threw it in Cody's direction. Cody leapt back to dodge the water and laughed even harder before he turned to flip the burgers.

Jessie laughed too but then slowly got up from her seat. She walked casually to the swimming pool, grabbed a filled water gun, and put it behind her back. Walking slowly on her tip toes, Jessie got right behind Cody and began to squirt water on his back.

Cody jumped from the cold water and whirled around to see Jessie laughing at him.

Loren watched them and was in shock. She couldn't believe that Jessie sprayed him with water when she had just met him. She didn't know how Cody would react either. He had a short temper when they met at the bar and hoped that wasn't his normal persona.

Cody pointed at Jessie with the spatula. "This means war!" he yelled.

Quick as lighting, Cody set the spatula on the table, grabbed Jessie, threw her over his shoulder, and walked towards the swimming pool.

Jessie began to kick and scream. "Don't you dare Cody. Don't. Cody don't!"

Sheena began to bark and ran towards the pool with them.

At first everyone was stunned and then laughed when Cody lifted Jessie into the air, leaned her over the edge, and she splashed into the pool.

Jessie surfaced and took a big breath. She jumped up and screamed, "I can't believe you did that!"

She splashed water at Cody and Sam got a bucket and tried to help too. Cody ran back towards the house and was laughing hysterically.

Jessie stepped out of the pool hugging herself and shivering. She grabbed a towel off a chair and dried a moment before she disappeared into the house. She didn't say a word.

Loren was astounded. She couldn't believe that Cody had the nerve to throw Jessie into the water. She couldn't believe it at all. "Oh, my gosh, Cody. She is going to retaliate you know."

"Bring it on. I just hope your sister is one who can take it as well as she gives it out," Cody answered as he petted Sheena's head.

Loren laughed, "I hope so to or you're on your own to find a date."

"I never thought of that," Cody whispered.

Jessie came back just as the steaks and burgers were being set on the table. She had changed into dry clothes and put her wet hair up into a bun. She did not look at anyone, grabbed a plate, and filled it before she started to eat.

Everyone ate in silence. There were glances between Loren, Erik and Cody and giggles from Sam. Finally Sam started to laugh and couldn't stop.

Sam said, "Aunt Jessie your hair looked like a big bird's nest when you fell into the water. It was so funny. I hope Cody does it again."

Jessie glared at Sam. "He better not do it again." She turned her direction towards Cody. "Paybacks are a bitch."

Sam gasped. "Aunt Jessie, that's not a nice word. You shouldn't say that."

"Sorry sweetheart. But I meant what I said." She looked back at Cody and scowled at him.

Cody put an entire asparagus spear in his mouth. When he was done chewing, he swallowed hard and took a drink of tea. "Hey, you started it. I just finished it."

Jessie took a bite of fruit salad and looked at him with a sarcastic smirk. "You didn't finish anything. It has just started."

Loren and Erik inhaled loudly and started to laugh. Loren looked from Jessie to Cody and back to Cody again. "I told you she'd retaliate. I know her better than you. She's my big sister and I have endured a lot over the years. You better watch your back Cody."

Cody cut at his steak and didn't look up. "I'm not scared."

K A Neemeyer

Chapter 17

*L*oren listened to the gravel beneath the tires and felt like it was going to put her in a trance. The crunching noise along with the engine of Erik's truck, was almost too relaxing. But she let the noises continue to soothe her while she looked around her surroundings.

It was the perfect kind of day to take a scenic drive and escape from everything else. Erik and Loren had packed a lunch, shut off their phones, and left before anyone in the house had gotten up that morning. Placing a note on the counter, Loren told Jessie and Sam to take care of themselves and that she would be back in the evening. She knew Jessie didn't have any plans which made today a good day to leave.

Erik pointed out the window and Loren turned to see a big bear catch a fish from the lake.

Within seconds he was already devouring it before the fish had time to slip from the bear's grip and dive back into the water.

Loren watched as the bear swallowed the last of the fish before she turned her direction towards Erik. She thought he looked relaxed and happy to be where he was. His hands gripped the steering wheel softly and he smiled as he glanced around at the scenery as he drove. Loren smiled to herself and liked to see him so happy.

Turning off the main road, Erik drove on a weathered beaten dirt road and parked under some trees. He slapped the steering wheel with his hand.

Loren jumped. "You scared me. You do that all the time." She grinned at him and grabbed a camera. "Ready to go for a walk?"

Erik laughed, grabbed them each a water, and shut his door quietly behind him. "What direction do you want to go? I think we should stay closer to the road so we don't have any troubles with animals."

"I agree. Let's head towards the lake. I bet we could see a lot of stuff there."

They walked in silence and Loren listened to the wind as it blew into the trees. When she looked up, she could see the branches swaying with the breeze which left moving shadows on the ground below. She imagined a bird's nest nestled high in the tree and imagined its babies swayed to sleep with the lulling movement.

Below the sound of the trees, Loren could hear a stream leading towards the lake, but as she looked beside her, the foliage was too thick to see anything. Nonetheless, the sound of the cascading water made her want to push through the thick branches and vines to view, what she imagined, a beautiful sight. She listened to the water and let it take her thoughts.

After walking a few minutes, the lake came into view. Loren exhaled loudly when she saw the splendor it displayed.

The reflections on the water captivated her while the water hitting the beach softly called her to it. Birds were dipping into the lake to catch a small fish or insects and a fisherman reeled in his line. There were large rocks, on one side of the lake, which big horn sheep were balancing on while a group of bison were grazing in the distance. It was all picturesque.

Erik grasped her hand and squeezed. "This was a good idea. I think we both needed this."

Loren sat down and continued to look out at the lake and all of its attractions. "It is so beautiful. I can't get over how nature can take my breath away. I mean, I see a lot from the windows of my house, but this is so much more. It's . . . it's perfect."

Erik sat beside her. "I've lived here all my life and still can't get enough of it. I'm happy I have someone to share it with me now."

Loren leaned her head on Erik's shoulder and sighed. "I'm happy too. I think we're going to make a lot of new and good memories together. And I like the idea that it is with you."

"I kind of hoped you'd like that idea."

"Yes Erik, I do. I have realized a lot the last few days. I've opened my eyes more and have really noticed how you treat Sam and me. And even Jess. I can see what a wonderful man you are and am ready to move forward."

"You are just now seeing this? I've been trying to show you how much you mean to me for over a year. I know it wasn't love at first sight for you, but it was pretty close to that for me."

Loren stared out at the mountains behind the lake. When she squinted, she could see some snow on top of the mountain tops and it made her shiver. "Erik I know. I know that you're the right man for me. Sorry it took me so long to figure it out."

"All that matters is that you finally have."

They sat and admired their surroundings for a few minutes before either of them spoke. Loren tried to memorize everything she was seeing while she was next to Erik. She felt happy on the inside and finally was at peace with her decision to marry again. Turning towards him, she watched his expression change with every direction he turned. He would smile as he watched the birds dive into the water and would get a more serious expression as he watched two sheep butt heads.

Loren watched the sheep for a few moments and her thoughts went to Sam and Jessie. "Do you think we should give them a call at the house? I'm sure their up by now. I kind of feel guilty expecting Jess to watch Sam without any notice."

"You can if you want, but I think it'll be fine. You said Jess was just going to hang around the house today."

"Yeah, but it's different to think you're going to hang around the house without a ten year old bugging you," Loren said.

Erik shielded his eyes from the sun and looked across the lake. "She should have expected that when she moved in. Speaking of that, when is she ever going to move out? I'm not trying to rush her, or you, I'm just wondering."

Loren frowned. "It still bothers you, doesn't it?"

"I guess it does a little. I understand why she's there, I just want to know how long."

Loren had a feeling where the conversation was going and didn't like it. "I don't know. I haven't asked. I think she's still trying to get her brain wrapped around everything. She'd been with Derik for a long time and then it ended like it did. I'm not forcing her out anytime soon. I hope you understand that."

"Okay. Then when do you want to set a date to get married?" He paused. "Do we have to plan our wedding and living together around how long it's going to take your sister to get her act together?" Erik asked with a condescending tone.

Loren shook her head. "Why are you doing this? We're in all this beauty and you're ruining it." She stood up, stretched her back, and looked back down at Erik. "Jess is very important to me. She practically raised me when we were kids. I see her as more than just a sister. I look up to her and I feel I owe her for all she did for me when we were little. I mean, my parents were gone the majority of our childhood. If it wasn't for Jess, I don't know."

Erik stood up and looked Loren in the eyes. He spoke softly. "I know all of this Loren. I just want to know when it's ever my turn to have you to myself. It's always been one thing or another. You not wanting to hurt Sam's feelings, you wanting to get the shop situated, and now Jess."

Loren picked up a stick and threw it into the water. "I don't want to do this right now. I thought we were coming here to enjoy a day together. Not to have you drill me about how I'm running *my* life." She began to walk back towards the truck and couldn't believe how the situation had turned so fast. She couldn't understand what the rush was to get married. They hadn't been dating for five years or even two. Loren had enough. "Let's just head home. I'll kick Jess out of the house, tell Sam to suck it up, and close the shop. I'll open my house doors to you and be a little house wife to have your meals ready every night. I'll wear sexy lingerie and send Sam off to a friend's as much as possible." She turned back and glared at Erik. "Is that what you want? Will that make you happy?"

Erik stared at the ground and kicked at the grass. "That wasn't my intention. I didn't mean to bring any of that up. It just kind of . . . slipped. I want planning on . . . oh hell. Can we start over?"

Loren rolled her eyes. "I don't think so. I have a lot to think about."

Erik took a few steps to catch up with her. "Loren come on. I didn't want to ruin the day. I didn't plan on talking about any of it. Cut me some slack, will ya."

Shrugging her shoulders, Loren continued back to the truck. "I don't know Erik. Maybe things aren't in tune for us or maybe it's just going too fast. I don't have an answer for you. I don't know when we'll get married. I don't know."

Erik caught up to Loren and twisted her around so she was looking at him. "Stop it. Just stop it. Every time the marriage thing comes up, it turns into a fight. I don't know why that happens. Do you want to get married Loren? Do you?"

Loren could see the sincerity in Erik's eyes and she sighed. "Erik. I love you. I love you and want to marry you. I just can't give you a day. We can sit down and look at a calendar and figure it out. But I can't tell you right now. Do you have a calendar in your truck or on your phone? Let's go figure it out."

"Are you being sarcastic or serious?"

Loren looked at the ground, nodded her head, and was overwhelmed. "I'm being serious. Now, let's go."

They slowly walked back towards the truck and Loren felt deflated. She listened to the stream hidden by the plants and she slumped her shoulders. She wanted to see the stream. She wanted to enjoy the day. She wanted to have a beautiful day with Erik. Why did it have to get ruined, and so quickly?

Was it just her having trouble with all of it? Was she trying to sabotage her chance at a marriage again? Loren was confused and hurt. She wanted to be home already and go to her room and be alone. She had wanted the day to be alone with Erik, but now she just wanted to be alone. Maybe she would take a long bath with some candle light and soft music. Maybe she should work in the garden and take her frustrations out on the weeds. Maybe she should go for a drive by herself and get lost.

Banging the door shut, Loren turned on her phone. "I'm gonna call them. Okay?" she said seriously but with a sarcastic tone.

"Whatever. It doesn't matter anymore. Let them know we're on our way back . . . already."

Loren felt guilty but also was mad for feeling guilty. Was it her fault he was rushing her? Did she need to kick Jess out of the house? She felt confused and exhausted.

Erik slammed his door and started the truck. Just as soon as the engine began to move its cylinders and pistons, he shut it down just as fast. He slammed his hand against the steering wheel and stared out the windshield. "This is dumb. I love you. You love me. What's the problem here? Why can't we figure this out like adults? Why does it have to turn into an argument every time?"

Loren watched as Erik slouched in the seat. He looked as frustrated as her. She groaned. "I don't know Erik. I do know that I want to get married, but not on the time table you keep giving me. What's the rush? We're an exclusive couple and I'm wearing your ring. I'm not looking for anyone else and don't plan on it. Why the hurry? Why can't it just happen as it happens?"

Erik fidgeted with the steering wheel and spoke softly. "I thought when a woman got engaged that it was a whirl wind to get the wedding day planned. I haven't even seen you buy a wedding magazine. I haven't seen you look into a shop window, to look at a dress, when we stroll down the street or even ask me what kind of cake I'd want. You haven't put any, I mean, any effort into wanting to be married. When I don't see any of it, I guess I feel like I'll never marry you. That's why I keep asking."

Loren felt horrible. She never thought of it that way. He was right. She hadn't even thought of wedding plans. Why hadn't she? "Erik, I . . . ." She stopped mid-sentence and didn't know how to answer him.

Erik started the truck and put it into reverse. "Just forget about it. I guess it'll figure itself out eventually and I'll wait until then. I'm not giving up on us. Just so you know."

Loren's heart felt like it was going to break. Both for Erik and herself.

Chapter 18

*J*essie stepped down the stairs and Loren and Sam were in awe. She was wearing a royal blue colored dress that flared at the waist and had an open back. The material draped beautifully and the soft satin looked shiny and flawless. Her black hair looked like silk with it being pulled back and little ringlets of hair falling gracefully towards her neck. She wore a small amount of make-up except for her red lips. She looked exquisite.

Loren sighed. "Wow Jess. You look awesome. You'll definitely be the princess at the ball. No one will be able to take their eyes off you."

Jessie twirled around in a small circle and smiled. "I have to admit that I think I look pretty good too. I feel beautiful in this dress."

Loren stood up and softly hugged her sister, afraid to wrinkle her dress. "You look beautiful. I need to get my camera," she said and headed towards the kitchen cabinet. "You can't leave until I have at least a hundred pictures of you."

Sam hadn't moved from her seat and stared at Jessie. "You're an angel."

Loren smiled at Sam and looked back at Jessie. "She is, isn't she? Now pose for me."

Jessie gave a few quick smiles and then grabbed her purse. "I need to get going."

Loren raised her eyebrows. "Cody's not picking you up? That's just wrong."

Jessie rolled her eyes. "It's not a big deal Loren. We agreed to meet at the dance so I could leave when I wanted to."

"He still should have picked you up," Loren said.

"It's not a prom date. It's just a casual date that happens to be a thing for his work."

Sam slowly walked towards Jessie and reached out to touch her dress. "It looks so soft. Can I wear it when I'm big enough?"

Jessie giggled. "Yes sweetie. You can when you're bigger. Love you guys, but I need to go. Thanks for helping me get ready. I couldn't have done it without you," she said and headed out the door. Very carefully she got into her vehicle and made sure her dress was completely in before she shut the door. Waving good-bye, she headed down the long drive way.

Loren and Sam waved as Jessie drove away and continued waving until all they could see was dust flying on the road.

Loren put her arm around Sam's shoulder and sighed. Jokingly she said, "She's growing up so fast."

Sam giggled and turned to go into the house. "You're weird mom." Plopping down on the couch, Sam hugged a pillow. "What do you want to do now? Are we going to wait up until Aunt Jessie gets home? Does she have a curfew?"

Loren smiled. "No. She doesn't have a curfew. She's older than me if you remember. And no, you're not staying up until she gets home. I have no idea when that will be. But I will allow you to stay up for a while. How about some popcorn and a movie?"

Loren and Sam snuggled up on the couch with a big bowl of hot popcorn and began to watch their favorite movie. Loren noticed Sam was asleep half way through the film and she felt her eyes getting heavy too. Her eyes didn't open again until she heard the door open to the front of the house. When she peaked over the back of the couch, she couldn't believe what she saw.

Jessie stood in the doorway with a look of fear and shock on her face. The shoulder strap to her dress was ripped and hanging. She had blood smeared across her cheek and shoulder.

Loren quickly and softly pushed Sam to the side and rushed to the door. "What happened? Did Cody do this?"

"No I didn't do anything," Cody said from the door as he stepped inside. "This is the courtesy of . . . Derik?"

Loren looked at Cody and saw he had a black eye and a split lip. His knuckles looked swollen and there was dried blood on them. "What the hell is going on?" she asked.

Jessie remained in the same spot and swayed side to side. Her eyes looked glassy and she looked pale.

Cody took her by the hand and led her to a chair in the living room. "I'll explain everything, but I think Jessie needs some attention first."

Loren ran to the bathroom and grabbed the first aid kit. Then she grabbed a roll of paper towels and a warm bowl of water. Placing it all on the table, she led Jessie there also and began to see if the dried blood was hers or someone else's. As she cleaned the blood from Jessie's cheek, she found a scratch mark. Dabbing it with hydrogen peroxide, before she put some first aid ointment on it, Loren held back her tears. She didn't need to be emotional and make the situation any worse. She looked back at Cody and frowned. "Now can you tell me what's going on? I can't believe this happened. How?"

Cody joined them at the table and held Jessie's hand. He glanced up at Loren and looked exhausted. "Where do I start? Jessie and I met in front of the coffee shop to walk together to the dance. She was gorgeous. I mean gorgeous. I felt like the luckiest guy ever. We started . . ."

Loren grew impatient. "Yeah. Yeah. You walked to the dance. How'd this happen?" she asked pointing towards Jessie's dress.

Cody shook his head and looked down at his knuckles. "As I was saying . . . We were walking to the dance and it was the perfect evening. The moon was shining, there was a soft breeze, and I had a beautiful woman beside me. Anyways, we got to the dance and were enjoying ourselves. At least, I was. We danced a couple dances and laughed a lot. We were sitting at our table when, out of nowhere, a guy pushes me out of my seat. I turn around to stand up and a fist connects with my mouth."

Loren couldn't believe what she was hearing. No one thought that Derik would come back for a second round of messing with Jessie. Loren tried to concentrate on her sister and was happy when she wiped her shoulder that there were no scratches or cuts on it.

She glanced at Jessie's face and saw she still had a look of shock. She wasn't shaking or crying, but somehow seemed far away with her thoughts. Loren wished she could take the pain of what happened away from her and see her smiling as she had been before she left.

Sam's head peeked over the top of the couch and her sleepy eyes tried to adjust to what was going on. "Hey Aunt Jessie. You're home already? What time is it?"

Loren gave a worried glance at Cody and he nodded his head and stood up to go and look out a window. Loren was pleased he understood what she meant and headed towards Sam. She steered her towards the stairs and tried to keep her from looking too close at Jessie or Cody. "It's late. You need to head to bed and we'll talk in the morning."

"But mom, I want to talk to Aunt Jessie."

"Tomorrow, young lady. Tomorrow. Now, head to bed missy."

Sam dragged herself up the stairs and Loren heard her fall onto her bed. Satisfied she wouldn't have to worry about Sam seeing the mess, Loren headed back to the table and held Jessie's hands in hers. "How you doing sis? Do you want to talk about it yet?"

Jessie looked up at Loren and had tears in her eyes. "Why? Why'd he do this? Why?"

Loren squeezed her hands. "I don't know. I don't know how he even would have known where you were. I thought he headed out of town after being released from jail?"

"I don't know Loren," Jessie said sarcastically. "I guess I didn't keep track of him. I didn't know that I had to. I thought I was done with him. I thought it was over. I thought he would be out of my life. I thought I could move on with my own life." She took a deep breath and stared at the floor. "I was so embarrassed. I felt horrible for Cody." She looked over at Cody and more tears swelled in her eyes. "I'm so sorry. I shouldn't have even gone with you. It was all a big mistake."

Cody knelt in front of her and touched her knee. "Hey. It wasn't a big mistake. It was one of the best nights of my life. I loved having you next to me. I loved having your company. We had fun, didn't we?"

"Yeah. Until . . ."

Cody cut her off. "No. We had a good night. That's it. We'll stop the night at the moment when you about sprayed your champagne from your nose.

Remember that? I was telling a joke about the old man at the circus?"

Jessie tried to smile. "Yeah. I remember. That was a terrible joke."

Cody grinned. "It must not have been that bad the way you reacted. Anyways, that's where our date ended. Okay?"

Jessie looked at her torn shoulder strap and tried not to cry again. "Okay."

Loren respected Cody even more than she had before. He was being so kind to Jessie and trying to make her feel better when he was the one with a black eye and swollen lip. Loren grabbed some fresh paper towels and dipped them in the warm water. She began to dab at his lip and it began to bleed again. "I'm sorry Cody. I was trying to help."

Cody touched the back of his hand to his mouth and looked at it. He stood up and leaned on the counter. "You wanted to make me bleed more?" he said teasingly.

Loren went to the freezer and grabbed a couple of ice packs. She wrapped them each in a towel and placed one on his hand and had him hold the other one to his eye. "If I wanted to make you bleed, I wouldn't pick such a tender spot. I'd pick my own spot to make you bleed," she said back to him teasingly.

"Ouch. I won't get on your bad side," he said and tried not to laugh from the pain of his lip.

Jessie stood up and went to grab a beer from the fridge. She already seemed more relaxed and started to act like herself again. "Thanks guys. Cody, you really are a nice guy and Loren, thank you for not freaking out on me."

Loren gestured for a beer for her and Cody too. "Hey, not a problem. I've seen bigger scratches on you from when we were kids. And some of those scratches came from my own finger nails."

Jessie giggled and handed them each a beer. "I remember those days. You were a pain in the neck."

"Ha-ha. Very funny. Now can someone tell me the rest of the story?" Loren asked.

Cody and Jessie looked at each other and Jessie began to speak. "Well, Cody got knocked off his chair and then Derik punched him in the mouth. But Cody got up faster than a bear and hit Derik right in the nose. Then Derik got him in the eye and Cody got Derik in the jaw. But Cody didn't stop. He hit him in the stomach and ribs and cheek. Derik didn't have a chance." Jessie looked at Cody and then back at Loren. "He's tougher than he looks. That's for sure." She took a drink and licked her lips to moisten them with the beer. "Finally, some other guys at the party pulled Cody off Derik. They called the cops and Derik got arrested . . . again." Jessie started to giggle. "The funny part was that one of the officers was at my house the last time Derik was arrested. He had looked at Derik and said, 'You're not too smart now are you?' It was so funny."

Loren laughed. She was happy that Derik was behind bars again. And now that it happened twice in less than a month, she was sure he would be there for quite a while. "Well, he can't say that it was his first offense." Loren looked at Jessie's cheek and dress. "How did you get scratched and your dress torn if Derik didn't do it?"

Jessie looked at Cody and grinned. "That was actually Cody's fault."

Loren was confused. "Cody's? How?" she asked.

"Well, I wanted to get a whack at Derik and so I slapped him in the face. Derik came back at me with his fist and Cody pulled me back by my shoulder strap. His fingernails must have got me when he pulled me back. But if he wouldn't have, I would've had a lot more than just a little scratch."

"Hey, I grabbed whatever I could. I saw the rage in Derik's eyes and knew he wasn't going to stand there and let you slap him without coming back at you. You should feel lucky I didn't grab your hair," he said smiling at Jessie.

Jessie smiled back. "No. *You're* lucky you didn't grab my hair."

Loren drank her beer and watched them converse. She shook her head and found it fascinating how it changed from when the three of them had first met compared to how they were now. She watched as they joked around with each other about how Cody hit like a girl and how Jessie should have punched Derik instead of slapping him.

Jessie finished the last of her beer and stretched. "This has been one heck of a date. Thanks for that Cody. But I'm getting pretty tired. I'm gonna head to bed if that's alright with the two of you?"

Cody nodded his head. "I understand. You need your beauty rest."

Jessie rolled her eyes, gave them each a hug, and headed up the stairs. "Ha-ha. Thanks again for saving my butt."

"Anytime," Cody said and turned to sit at the table. He looked towards Loren and got a serious expression. "You're not going to head to bed too? Are you? I'm still pretty pumped up from the fight. There's no way I could go to bed anytime soon."

Loren looked at the clock above the kitchen sink. "I can stay up a while, but not too long. I have to work in the morning."

"Sweet. Thanks. Do you have something to drink other than beer? It's not tasting too good right now. How about some coffee or tea?"

Loren went into the kitchen and started a pot of decaffeinated coffee for the two of them. "Want some cake to go with it? We have some chocolate cake with whip cream icing."

"Sure. I can't pass on that. Do you think your sister will be alright? I didn't plan for the evening to end like this. I was hoping for a kiss on the cheek and maybe getting her to go out again sometime."

Loren cut a couple pieces of cake and brought them to the table. "She's pretty tough. Did I ever tell you that she raised me? Well, we had our parent's, but they weren't around too much. We had a butler and maid do most of the work around the house. Although, I felt like Jessie was my mom and sister, as far as I'm concerned. Needless to say, we're not too close to our parent's. We both feel like they picked their careers and money over us."

"That's too bad. I'm sorry to hear that. At least you had each other. I, myself, have three other siblings and I was the youngest. I guess you could say that I was kind of spoiled."

Taking a bite of her cake, Loren wondered if all his siblings displayed red hair like him. "Was your family pretty close?"

"Oh yeah. We did everything together. Now about Jessie. Do you think that she'll go out with me again? I really enjoyed her company. And from what I saw, she seemed to enjoy mine too. Unless she's an awesome actress and was faking it."

"Jessie has never faked an emotion. If she looked like she was having fun, then she was having fun. I don't know about the date thing though. That's something you'll have to ask her. How do you think that Derik found out where you were?"

"That, I have no idea. He seemed to come out of nowhere. The only thing I can think of is that he's been stalking her. I know that sounds scary, and it is."

Loren shivered when she thought of Derik spying on them. She heard the coffee finishing brewing and went to get them each a cup. "That gives me the willies. I don't like the thought of that. This is my home. I don't like the idea of someone spying on us here."

"I wouldn't either. But I don't think you'll have to worry about him for a while. I think the judge will keep him behind bars," he said.

Her thoughts suddenly went to Erik. "Can I ask you a question?"

"Sure. What's on your mind?" Cody asked.

"Erik. What do you think of him?"

"Seems like a good guy. Why do you ask?"

"Well, he asked me to marry him quite a while ago. He pointed out that I hadn't even started with the wedding plans or even set a date. Is that weird?"

"A little. I thought women got crazy when they were asked. I mean with all the arrangements and colors and stuff. At least the two I was engaged to did. They had stuff picked out within hours."

"Do you think it's because I don't want to get married that I'm not *getting crazy*?" Loren asked not knowing how he'd answer. She was even a little scared what he would think.

Cody sat and pondered the question. He took a couple bites of his cake and sipped on his coffee. "I don't know how to answer that. There could be a few reasons. One of them could be that you haven't let go of the idea of being married to your late husband. Another one could be that you're not an excitable woman when it comes to shopping. And maybe another one could be that you're not as in love with him as you thought. I don't know."

Loren sat back in her chair and stared at Cody. "I don't know either. I guess I'll start shopping and see how it feels. I think I'm just scared."

"Scared you might lose him too?" Cody asked.

She felt tears stream down her face. "You're right."

K A Neemeyer

Chapter 19

*L*oren handed her customer his change. She looked at the long line of customers waiting to be served and was pleased. She liked that she had a good name in the town for her coffee and that her customers kept coming back.

She had some regulars that would order their coffee and leave, while others would sit in the shop for hours. There were people on computers and others that read a few chapters from their favorite book. There were some that just stared out the window and daydreamed and others that chatted with a friend. Whichever way they drank their coffee, she was happy that they were happy.

Looking around, she loved the soft hum of the peoples' voices. She loved the smell of the coffee and the sound of the steam while making a latte or other frothy drink. She loved the smell of the pastries and how her customers were so comfortable in her shop. Loren took a deep breath and smiled.

Glancing down, Loren stared at her engagement ring and wondered if Cody was right. Was she afraid of losing Erik? Was she scared that she would give him her heart, her whole heart, and something bad would happen to him too?

The more she thought about it, the more it made sense. That's why she pushed off the wedding. That's why she picked arguments to postpone any idea of getting married. That's why she hadn't even thought of a dress or decorations or where to have the reception.

"Excuse me," a customer called to get her attention.

Loren shook her head and tried to push the thoughts away. "I'm sorry. What can I get you today?"

As the customer ordered, Loren had to stare at his mouth to concentrate on what he was saying. She suddenly didn't want to be there. She wanted to call Erik and tell him why she'd been acting so odd about the wedding. She wanted him to hold her and make everything alright.

But that wasn't going to happen right now. The day had just started and she was there for the long haul. Amber was gone for a family gathering and another employee was sick and another one was at college classes. So she was stuck there and there was no one else to take her place.

Loren knew there was a stack of paperwork to go through, which meant she would be there well after closing time. She pushed a strand of hair from her face and exhaled. She wanted to leave, but instead smiled and filled the next order.

After the morning rush had been given their steaming cups of coffee and pastries, Loren speed walked to her office to make a phone call. She immediately dialed Erik's number and hoped he would be available. She couldn't wait to tell him what she finally figured out.

"Well good morning Loren. It's good to hear your sweet voice so early in the day. What's up?"

Loren found herself speechless. She didn't know how to put how she felt into words.

"Hello?" Erik asked. "Are you there?"

She took a deep breath and spoke, almost in a whisper. "I know why I've had such trouble about us getting married."

"Really? I'm all ears." Erik responded.

"Cody and I were talking the other night and he helped me figure it out."

Erik grunted. "Cody huh. You've been talking about our love life to Cody?"

"Now come on. You know it's all innocent. If it wasn't for him I . . . I wouldn't have figured out the reason." She took a deep breath and nodded her head to reassure herself she was doing the right thing. "It's because I'm afraid of losing you like I did Craig. I'm afraid that if I give you all of me, that something bad will happen and I'll have to relive those same emotions again. I don't think I can do that. I think I'd have to go to a loony house."

"Ah Loren. You are such a sweet woman. I'm glad you figured it out, but what do we do about it? I can't see into the future, just as you can't." He paused a second. "All I can say is that I will love you with all of my heart and soul. I'll be beside you and we will get through anything that happens. I can't say that nothing will happen to me, but I think we should enjoy the time we have together. Don't you think so?"

Loren had tears running down her cheeks. She knew he meant what he said. "You're right. I've been wasting the time that we could have together already. Why don't we meet tonight and set a date. I'll get some magazines and start calling caterers and bakers. I know Jessie will do our flowers, so that's taken care of. And then this weekend Jessie and Sam and I will go look at dresses."

"Loren, I never thought I would hear sweeter words."

"I'm sorry it took me so long," she whispered and wiped the tears running down her cheeks.

"I guess I owe Cody a beer for helping you realize all of this. I'm so happy to hear it all, but I have a group of men waiting for my instructions. So . . . I'll talk to you tonight?"

"Yes. Oh yes. I love you Erik. Talk to you later."

She hung up the phone and sat back in her chair. She felt dizzy with excitement and so many other emotions. Smiling, she wiped her face and looked in a mirror she had hung on the side of her desk to make sure she didn't look like a mess before she went back out to her customers. Satisfied she looked alright, she stood up, put her hands up in the air momentarily from feeling successful, and headed back to greet her customers.

The rest of the day seemed to fly by. She couldn't stop smiling. It was like her life was finally going to begin again. Her heart felt like it was going to burst with excitement. She couldn't wait to get started with her life with Erik and knew she was ready.

She needed to drown out the ideas of losing him. If she continued to think that way, she would never have happiness. She needed to live in the moment and enjoy what she had while it was in front of her.

When the shop finally closed and the door was locked, Loren decided the paperwork could wait. She needed to see Erik and begin her life with him in a new light. And she needed to start right now. She knew she wanted to start a new chapter with him and enjoy every moment she could.

Instead of driving home, she headed to Erik's house. When he opened the door, Sheena was just as excited to see her as Erik was. Erik pulled her into his arms and breathed in the smell of her perfume. Then he pulled her away from him and stared into her eyes.

Loren's heart skipped a beat from his gaze. She knew she was making the right choice and hugged him tight. "I love you Erik Fisher. And I'm excited to become Mrs. Loren Fisher."

Erik held her tight and moaned. "I can't tell you how happy that makes me. There were so many times that I thought I would lose you. I didn't know if you would ever want to be married or be with me." He hugged her even tighter. "I love you too Loren Quinn, soon to be Loren Fisher."

Loren felt tears run down her face for the second time that day. She wiped them away, pulled away from him, and looked into his eyes. "I mean it.

I'm ready. I'm ready to spend the rest of my life with you. I'm ready for you to move into my house and make it our home. I'm ready for Sam to cuddle up to you and watch a movie. I'm ready to create new memories as a family."

Erik kissed her hard. He pulled her tightly to him again. He kissed her passionately and ran his fingers up and down her back.

Electricity ran through her body from his kisses. She felt a wave of heat between them that continued to get hotter from every moment they were near each other. She wrapped her arms around him and enjoyed every sensation from his touch.

Sheena began to bark and jump beside them. They pulled apart and both began to laugh.

Erik said, "I guess she's getting jealous. I think she wants you to give her some attention too."

Loren laughed harder. She knelt down to receive slobbery kisses on her cheek from Sheena and wiped them off as she stood back up. "Well, let's get down to business."

Erik gave her a mischievous look. "What kind of business are you talking about Loren?"

Loren felt another wave of heat flow through her body. She was tempted to throw her arms around him and fulfill her desires. "Erik, you're making this difficult. I meant to set a wedding date."

225

He grabbed her hands and looked into her eyes. "We can take care of both. Can't we? I mean, we are alone."

Loren looked around the room and couldn't resist the temptation. She wrapped her arms around Erik and kissed him with such passion, she thought she was going to fall from the dizziness.

He responded to her kiss and lifted her into the air and Loren wrapped her legs around his waist. He didn't break their kiss, but carefully maneuvered them across the room and into his bedroom. There he gently lowered her to the bed and put his weight on top of her. Again, without breaking the connection of their kiss.

Loren suddenly felt hot and pondered momentarily on the thought of removing some of her clothing. But she couldn't with Erik on top of her and she didn't want to stop kissing him.

Their kisses grew even more passionate and neither of them could get enough. Erik ran his fingers through her hair and down her ribs. He tugged at her shirt and Loren arched her back to have the shirt pulled from under her.

Erik rolled to the side of her and started to touch her stomach with the tips of his fingers. Loren felt goose bumps raise from his touch. Her breathing got heavier and she became even hotter.

When Erik broke their connection and began to kiss her stomach, Loren thought she was going to go mad. She was breathing noisily and she could feel his mouth on her as her stomach rose and fell with each breath. She glanced down at him and saw a look of desire on his face which made her breathe even heavier yet.

Erik began to graze her hips with his hands and back up to her stomach. He was breathing heavily too which made Loren even more excited.

All of a sudden, Loren heard Sheena pant from beside the bed. Then she rested her head on the edge of the bed and stared at them.

Loren glimpsed over at her and started to laugh. "I can't do this with an audience." She said and sat up. She pulled her shirt back down and sat on the side of the bed.

Erik rolled onto his back and groaned. "Sheena. Sometimes I wonder about you. Thanks a lot girl."

"It's not her fault. She's used to snuggling in bed with you and I took her spot," Loren laughed.

"That habit is going to stop. She's not going to ruin the moment every time," Erik moaned.

Loren petted Sheena on the head. "Just look at her. She's adorable. Maybe we can get her to sleep with Sam when you move into the house."

Erik got a serious look on his face and sat up. "I never thought I'd hear you say that either. I'm so happy Loren. You make me happy."

"Thanks. You make me happy too," Loren said and blushed.

She got up from the bed and walked back into the living room. She plopped down on the couch and waited for Erik to join her. She heard him groan again before he finally stepped from the bedroom and joined her on the couch.

He said, "That wasn't right. I was prepared to spend at least an hour or more in there."

Loren smiled. "I'm sorry. The moment was lost with your dog staring at me."

"You mean, our dog?"

"Yes, our dog. Now do you have a calendar handy? We need to set a date before I get cold feet again."

Erik opened his lap top and clicked on a calendar. "Quick! Pick a day," he laughed. "I don't want you to change your mind." He cupped her face in his hand and gazed into her eyes. "I don't ever want you to change your mind," he said softly.

Loren felt electricity go through her body again. She was tempted to start again what they hadn't finished, but pushed the thought away. She needed to concentrate on a wedding date. They would have plenty of time to be with each other when he moved into the house.

After a forty five minute discussion about when family would be able to attend and what time of year would be the best, they finally agreed on a date. It would take place in less than four months and would be a fall wedding. Loren thought it would not be enough time, but Erik convinced her that they had waited long enough and that everything would fall into place.

Erik marked the date on his computer with bold lettering. Then he forwarded the date to Loren's phone and email. He started laughing. "Okay. I sent it to you too so you don't forget."

"Ha-ha. I better get going. I need to stop by the store to get some magazines for ideas and I need to tell Jess and Sam. They're going to be so happy."

"I hope so. But before you go I need one more thing."

"What's that?" Loren asked.

"One more kiss."

K A Neemeyer

Chapter 20

*T*he next morning Loren woke up in a wonderful mood. She stretched under her covers and then stared at her ring. She heard her door open and looked to see Sam grinning at her.

Sam said, "Good morning mom. I made a surprise for you."

Loren sat up in bed. "What's that Sammie bear?"

Sam walked through the doorway holding a tray. She had made Loren breakfast. "I thought you would want a good start to your day before we go shopping. We are going shopping right?"

"Yes, we're going shopping. But you have to remember the day is to shop for me, not you."

Sam set the tray on Loren's lap and moaned. "I know. But we can get me something, can't we?"

Loren looked at the tray and smiled. It had scrambled eggs, toast, orange juice, and a small vase with a purple flower in it. She was impressed. "You did this yourself Sammie? It looks wonderful."

Sam sat on the edge of the bed. "I did. I didn't even get any egg shells in the scrambled eggs," she said with a big grin on her face.

"You are growing up too fast. Thank you very much. What made you think of making me breakfast?"

Sam stared at the toast and licked her lips. "I just thought it would be nice. I saw how happy you were last night when you told us about Erik. It made me happy too. So I thought that I would start your day good. Did I do a good job?"

Loren handed her a slice of the toast. "You did awesome. I'm very proud of you. Did you know that?"

Sam shrugged her shoulders. "It's just breakfast."

"It's more than just breakfast. You are growing into such a wonderful young lady."

"Ah mom. Don't get mushy."

Loren took a bite of the eggs followed by a drink of her juice. "Is your Aunt Jess up yet?"

"I think she's in the shower. She was saying that she was going to call someone in to work so that we can shop all day. Isn't that great?"

Loren frowned. "I don't want her to miss work because of me."

Jessie walked into the room and fell down on the bed. "Hey, it's all good for me. I can't wait to see you in a wedding dress again. It's gonna be a good day. I can feel it."

With that, all three of them picked at the tray of food until all that was left was crumbs.

When they were finished, they got dressed and headed fifty miles east of town to find a place to shop. It was a bigger town with more selection and more wedding retailers.

They were all overwhelmed with the choices of dresses and accessories to go with them. Loren tried on two dozen gowns and at least three dozen veils. Sam and Jessie sat and waited to see each gown and gave her a thumbs up or down of what they thought. When Loren stepped out in her final choice, Jessie and Sam were speechless.

It was an oatmeal colored couture mousseline gown. It was a fit and flare style and was exquisite.

It exhibited wider shoulder straps that were embellished with small crystals and silver sequins.

The same embellishment went straight across the bodice area. Then the decoration began to twist around the dress's stomach and waist where it finally decreased in decoration as it cascaded down the dress. And a small amount of tangerine colored organza fabric peaked from the under the bottom layer of mousseline. The back of the dress was open down to the middle of the back where the sequins and crystals flowed down from there.

When Loren stepped up on the platform and turned to look at herself in the mirror, she began to tear up. She couldn't believe how the dress hugged her body like it was made just for her and how the details of the dress seemed to be perfectly placed. Besides that, the color of tangerine under the dress made it easy for her to decide on the color of the bridesmaids dresses.

While she was looking in the mirror, she could see Jessie and Sam watching her. Their expressions gave Loren joy that they loved it too. When they finally spoke, they couldn't say enough of how beautiful she looked and how well it fit. And then Sam asked if she would be able to wear it on her wedding day and Loren was overjoyed.

She felt beautiful in the dress and couldn't wait to get married so she could wear it again. She stood in front of the mirror for ten minutes before she finally stepped down from the platform and went to change her clothes.

Since the dress fit perfectly and she wasn't going to need any alterations, Loren bought the dress before she left the store. She wasn't even nervous when she signed for it. Instead, she was excited and anxious for Erik to see her come down the aisle.

After placing the dress gently in the back end of her Jeep, the three of them went to get a celebration lunch. They headed to a steak house where Loren and Jessie ordered a big steak and Sam ordered a burger and fries.

Loren chewed a big bite of her steak before she tried to talk. "Thanks for coming with me gals. It means more finding the dress with you two with me. I kind of wish I had mom to be here, but I don't even know where her and dad travel to anymore. Do you Jess?"

Jessie took a drink of her soda and shook her head. "I have no idea. The last time I heard from them, they were headed to Spain. I think that was a couple months ago."

Sam took a bite of a ketchup covered french-fry and had a confused look on her face. "Why do they travel so much? I think I've seen grandma and grandpa twice my entire life."

"That's just who they've always been and always will be. They're more into traveling the world than into their family. Sorry they're like that sweetheart," Jessie said.

Loren felt bad for her daughter. Sam came home a few times talking about her friends staying at their grandparent's for the summer or going on vacation with them. Every time she told a story about it, she had a sad expression on her face. "Sorry they're not like some of the other grandparents. I'm sure it's tough on you. But we didn't have them as parent's really either. That's why Jessie and I are so close. We grew up together and your Aunt Jessie took care of me more than my own folk's did."

Sam still looked confused. "Why'd they even have kids if they weren't going to be with them? Isn't that why married people have children? To be a family?"

Loren frowned. "It's not a perfect world Sammie. But I had Jessie so I had a good childhood."

Sam leaned over and hugged Loren's arm. "Thanks for being a good mom. I'm glad I have you as much as I do. When I have kids, I'll make sure to be with them as much as I can too."

Jessie and Loren looked at each other. They both had a look of sorrow and happiness at the same time. They were sorry Sam didn't have grandparent's like she wanted and happy she appreciated what she did have.

Loren patted Sam on the back. "Hey, you still have Grandma and Grandpa Quinn. I know you don't see them very much, but it's more than my folks. I guess it's still hard with them since they practically live across the Unites States from us."

Sam dipped another fry into her ketchup and smiled. "You're right. When do we get to see them again? Will they be at the wedding?"

"I don't know about that. I am marrying another man. I don't think they'd want to be there," Loren said.

"Well, can I ask them?"

"Of course you can. They're your grandparents. If you want them to come then we will ask." She paused. "But I think we'll call them before we send out an invitation," Loren added.

Sam seemed satisfied with Loren's answer and continued eating. When they were all full, they headed to another wedding boutique to look at more veils and some accessories for the reception hall and church.

A couple hours later, they were finally on their way home. Just as they got onto the interstate Loren got a phone call.

"Hi there Loren. This is Cody. Would Jessie happen to be around you anywhere close?"

Loren gave Jessie a playful grin and handed her the phone. "It's Cody. He wants to talk to you."

Jessie grabbed the phone and gave her a cynical look. "Hello?"

Loren tried to listen to the phone call, but Jessie leaned as far away as she could. Jessie smiled a few times and gave yes and no answers to what Cody said. When she hung up she stared out the window.

Loren slapped her on the shoulder. "What did he say? What'd he want?"

Jessie grinned and continued staring out the window. "Oh. He wanted to know if I'd go on another date with him."

"He did? What did you say?" Loren asked and was growing impatient with her sister's lack of interest in the conversation.

"I said I would. We're going to try and go out tomorrow night. Hopefully this time it won't end horribly."

Loren giggled. "It won't end badly. It wasn't your fault how it ended last time. Now that Derik's out of the picture, again, it should go more smoothly for you."

Jessie glanced at Loren and then looked back out the window and sighed. "I don't know. Maybe it's a sign that I shouldn't date right now. Maybe I need to get the rest of my life back in order before I try to see anyone."

Sam chimed in. "I think he's cool. I really liked it when he threw you in the pool. That was so funny."

Jessie looked back at Sam and wrinkled her lips. "That is another reason I shouldn't date him. What kind of guy throws his girlfriend in the pool?"

Loren laughed. "A guy who's not afraid of you. I think that's a good start."

K A Neemeyer

Chapter 21

*T*o help Jessie feel more comfortable, Loren and Erik joined her and Cody on their date. They decided to head to dinner and maybe go to a show afterwards. When they arrived to the restaurant they were amazed at the line of people waiting to be seated.

Erik smiled and walked up to the young woman that was in charge of seating. "I have a reservation for four under the name Erik Fisher."

Loren was impressed. She hadn't thought about it being so busy and having to get a reservation. She looked at Erik with admiration. She began to see him differently since he had properly proposed to her. It was like her eyes had been opened a little more to the wonderful man he was.

As they were led to their seats, Loren squeezed Jessie's elbow. "I'm falling in love with him more every day. What a guy to get us set up with a table."

Jessie grinned. "I'm impressed too."

Loren watched as Cody pulled Jessie's chair out for her to be seated. Before he seated himself, he squeezed her shoulder and smiled. Loren was impressed with both men. "Wow. We ladies are with two gentleman tonight."

Erik smirked. "We're not gentlemen the other days of the week?"

"You know what I mean. It seems extra special tonight." Loren responded.

She looked away from Erik and glanced around the room. She noticed the music playing in the background, along with the soft lighting, made the restaurant alluring. Loren looked around at the other guests and could see they felt the same way. Everyone looked satisfied to be where they were. Although, she could see a few couples that looked a little out of place. She figured it was either because it was their first date or because they had never been to a fine restaurant before. But overall, the mood was soft and inviting. It made Loren want to sit there for hours and just enjoy the atmosphere.

Erik held Loren's hand as he looked at his menu. He stared at the list of options intently like it was hard to decide what to have. He looked up at

Loren with a confused look. "What are you going to get? I don't know what I'm hungry for tonight." He paused. "But I know what I'm having for dessert. I'm going to have sweet kisses from you and maybe more."

Loren blushed. She looked towards Jessie and Cody to see if they had been listening. Neither one looked up, but they both had a smile on their face. "Erik. Don't say stuff like that in front of them," she whispered.

"Why not? They know that we're in love and getting married. I think it would be assumed that we kiss." Erik said with a smirk on his face.

Jessie began to giggle. "Yeah. I don't need to know what goes on behind closed doors. She is my sister and I don't want images like that in my head."

Cody agreed. "Me neither."

Erik shook his head and continued to look at his menu. He kept smiling until the waitress came to take their order.

After they had all decided what they would eat, Cody grabbed his glass of water and waved it in front of him. "I think this was a good idea. I don't know if I wanted to be alone with Jessie. The last time was a little eventful for my taste. This way I have back up."

Jessie punched him on the shoulder. "Hey. That wasn't my fault. It isn't like I asked Derik to show up and ruin the night. I was actually enjoying myself."

Cody sat back in his chair. "You act like it's surprising that you had fun."

"No . . . I . . . ." Jessie stammered.

Smiling, Cody winked at her. "Uh huh. Now I know how you really feel."

Jessie punched him on the shoulder a second time and scowled at him. "You know what I meant."

Loren couldn't be happier with the way they were interacting. They already acted like a couple with their teasing and flirting. And even though their first date ended badly, they still seemed like they wanted to keep trying. She was ecstatic for them. It was wonderful to have her sister smiling again. And it looked like an authentic smile. Not a fake one.

They continued with small talk until their food came to the table. Everyone breathed in the smells of the meat, vegetables, and pasta. It all looked wonderful. Everyone grabbed a fork and dug in. It was silence for a few minutes until they got a taste of the food.

Erik pointed his fork at Cody and had a serious expression. "Cody. I forgot to thank you."

Cody looked surprised. "Thank me? For what?"

"You talked some sense into my fiancé. It was you that finally opened her eyes to why she didn't want to get married."

"I did? When did I do that?" Cody asked.

Loren laughed. "You did something wonderful and you don't remember? That's funny."

Cody looked confused. "No really, what did I do. If I'm getting credit for something wonderful, I want to know what I did to deserve it."

"The night you and Jessie came home from the dance. You and I talked . . . ring a bell?" Loren asked.

"Oh. Now I remember. Wow. I'm awesome and didn't even know it." He looked towards Loren. "I guess you owe me big time then, right?"

Swallowing a bite of vegetables, Loren smiled. "I guess I do."

Jessie stared at all of them. "What are you all talking about?"

Erik chuckled. "You don't know? Cody saved the world. He's Superman."

Everyone laughed.

After they were done eating and their plates were taken away, they sat and sipped on a glass of wine. Jessie leaned into Cody and looked comfortable with him. Loren and Erik held hands and Erik massaged the top of her hand with his thumb. He glanced at her every few moments and looked at her with pure love. Loren felt her heart beat fast every time he looked her way.

Erik banged his knuckles on the table. "Well. I think we should get out of here and let someone else have a chance to sit down. Anyone up for taking a stroll in the park?"

Jessie and Cody nodded. Loren thought it was a nice thought too. It was a beautiful evening and there was no reason to be inside all night.

The men took care of the bill and Loren and Jessie went outside to wait. Loren gave her sister a hug. "I'm so happy that you and Cody are getting along so well. I think you two look kind of cute together."

Jessie closed her eyes for a moment. "I don't know what to do. I really like him but . . . I don't know if I'm ready to dive into another relationship. It's so soon after getting away from Derik. Isn't it?"

Loren thought for a second. "I don't think so. I think it's good for you to date to forget that jerk. You don't have to go through a mourning period for him. He doesn't deserve it."

"You're right. I don't know why I stayed with him anyways. It was stupid to stay in that relationship just because I didn't want to be alone. Who knows, I might have met Cody earlier."

Loren saw Erik and Cody coming towards the door. "I think you and Cody make a good couple. But it's not up to me. You need to decide that. They're on their way out and Cody looks really happy. I think he likes you as much as you do him."

Erik put his arm around Loren after he came outside. He kissed the top of her head and breathed in the smell of her hair. "I love how you smell. You wear the perfect perfume and use the perfect shampoo. It's intoxicating."

Cody snickered and leaned towards Jessie to smell her hair.

She pulled away and frowned. "I don't think we're in that place in our relationship just yet."

"So you admit we're in a relationship? That's good," Cody said. "I was hoping that you thought we were going somewhere like I did."

Jessie grabbed his hand and yanked. "Let's go for a walk. We'll talk about that stuff some other time. Okay?"

Loren and Erik giggled and followed them towards the park across the street.

When they stepped onto the sidewalk, Loren instantly felt at ease. She looked around and liked what she saw.

The city had recently added lamp posts that seemed like they came from the early nineteen hundreds. The sidewalk weaved within the park with benches placed to sit and rest or converse. The benches also looked like they had come out of an older era with the metal being crafted into different shapes and painted black. She liked how the way it looked made her feel like she was in a simpler time of taking walks and enjoying the scenery.

There was a flower garden with a bench right in the middle and bushes and trees planted throughout the entire area. But the best part for Loren was the gazebo. She liked how they had flower vines climbing the sides with white and red flowers blooming in the evening air. There were also little miniature lights twisted around the pillars that gave off a soft ambience. She wanted to go and dance under the stars displayed through slats of wood used as a roof.

She felt Erik lead her towards the gazebo and her heart began to race. When they stepped onto the threshold he turned towards her. He wrapped his arms around her and looked into her eyes. Loren almost began to cry from the love she saw.

Erik grinned. "You are the most wonderful woman. You're a wonderful mom too. And I'm so in love with you. I want to spend the rest of my life with you, and only you. I want to create so many memories that our grandchildren will never hear the same story twice. I want to hold you every day. I want to kiss your lips and feel your body next to me at night. I love you Loren."

She didn't know what to say. When she glanced back, she saw Jessie and Cody staring in awe. She looked back at Erik and felt tears slipping down her cheeks. "Wow. You are amazing. I've been so blessed to have you in my life. I was blessed once before, but I've been blessed even more. I don't know how you picked me but I'm glad you did."

Erik gently led her into the gazebo. Loren looked up at the rafters and saw stars twinkling beyond the flowers blooming above her head. It was the most beautiful sight. She could smell the scent of the flowers, from a soft breeze blowing through them, along with the scent of Erik's cologne. It seemed perfect to Loren. She was experiencing a spectacular moment of nature and love. This was something she would remember for the rest of her life. She didn't know if another sensation could ever compare to what she experienced at that instant.

Erik hugged her and they kissed.

Jessie stepped into the gazebo and broke the moment. "Um. Hey, we're going to go for a walk on our own and maybe go to a movie. I think you two need your own time right now anyways." She winked at Loren. "I won't wait up for you and you don't wait up for me."

Loren watched her sister step out of the gazebo and appreciated she was giving them some privacy. Besides, they needed to have their own time to themselves being a new couple. She continued to watch them until they walked into the flower garden and were out of sight. She grinned and grabbed Erik's hand and they began to walk slowly back towards the street. Loren sighed. "She ruined it. I was enjoying myself."

"That's okay. Their gone now and you and I can enjoy all the time together we want. Didn't you say that Sam was at her friend's for the night?"

"Yes she is but that doesn't mean that we have to . . . you know."

"I know. I was just meaning to enjoy our time together without interruptions. I wasn't expecting anything else Loren." He took her in his arms and squeezed gently. "Now what do you want to do?"

Loren thought for a moment and smiled. "Didn't you say something a while ago about teaching me to catch a frog in mid jump?"

Erik looked surprised. "Really? You want to go catch a frog?" He pointed towards her dress. "In what you're wearing? Really?"

"Why not? It all washes and it's a beautiful night."

Erik shook his head and smiled. "You never cease to amaze me." He glanced up at the night sky. "It's almost a full moon so they should be easier to see. I guess . . . let's go catch a frog."

Loren kissed him as he opened the door, to his truck, for her to get in. She smiled mischievously and then giggled. "Maybe we'll find other things to do in the moon light too."

Chapter 22

*E*rik decided to take Sam on a date of their own. He wanted to talk to her about him and Loren getting married and to have some quality time alone with just the two of them. They left early in the morning and planned on being gone the majority of the day.

Jessie also was going to be gone for the day and Loren was fully staffed at the coffee shop. That meant she had nowhere to go and the house was hers to have alone for the day. But as she thought about it, she didn't know what to do. She couldn't think of the last time she was had this time to herself.

Taking an extra few minutes to get out of bed, Loren ran herself a hot bath. She lit some candles and played "The Best of Mozart" on the stereo. She lowered herself into the water and let the music take all her thoughts away.

Finally, when her fingers felt wrinkly, she put on a robe and headed to the kitchen. There she cooked herself an omelet and toast and sat at the table to eat. After sitting for just a couple moments, she already did not like the quietness of the room. Looking around, she decided to turn the television on for the noise.

When she was done eating, she went to get dressed and grabbed her favorite necklace from the dresser. Once again, she began to think about Craig and how they had so many happy memories together. She hoped he was smiling down at her and knew that she was happy with her choice with Erik.

Her thoughts began to drift and she found herself thinking back to her time with Craig. It had been one of those rare times when Craig's parent's had asked to see Sam and went to spend the weekend with them. Taking advantage of their private time together they both called in sick to work. They jumped in to bed and decided they were going to stay there all day just being together. Then they made love, what seemed, countless times and had fallen asleep intertwined within each other's arms and legs.

They woke up to make love again followed by another nap. When it became dark outside, they finally decided to get some food and discovered that their legs were shaky and weak from being in bed all day. They laughed so hard they had tears in their eyes. Then they laughed again as they helped each other into the kitchen to find some food and, after finding some, they collapsed on the couch to eat. There, they fed each other and laughed some more.

It had been such a memorable day. They spent every second touching and kissing and holding each other. There was no other day like it and Loren would remember it until the day she died.

She would always remember the emotions and passion she had that day. She would remember how he smelled like cologne mixed with sweat and the desire he had for her. She would remember how his arms felt when he held her tight. But she would mostly remember how he loved her. How he looked into her eyes and it had felt like he had seen down to her very soul. She also remembered how he held her gaze and she couldn't look away from the love she saw in his expression.

Loren sighed and gently put the necklace back on the dresser. She continued to get dressed and found herself glancing back at the necklace numerous times. When she finished dressing, she grabbed it and held it up to the light.

The necklace hadn't been worn since Craig died. She hadn't been able to bring herself to put it around her neck thinking that she would feel a whirl wind of emotions she wouldn't be able to handle.

But today was different. She thought she might have the strength.

Loren knew that she needed to break through her emotions and move on to a new future. So slowly, she unclasped the chain and brought it up to her neck. Before she put it around it, she took a deep breath to calm her nerves to be ready for whatever happened. When she finally put the necklace on, she felt nothing. She felt nothing but the cold chain touching her skin.

Loren sighed a deep breath and sat on the edge of the bed. She didn't know if she was relieved or sad from the emotionless experience.

Shaking her head, Loren went back into the kitchen to get some coffee and touched the chain around her neck. When she sat down, she stared out the window at the mountains far away. It made her shiver with the thought of how it would feel to be at the very top of the tall mountain.

Loren laughed. She had just gotten more of an emotion looking at mountains that she wasn't near, then the necklace touching her skin that had taken years to put on.

Pushing the thought away, her thinking went to Erik and she was, once again, warm and happy. Happy that she finally burst through her wall of worry and was moving on with their wedding date.

She was glad that she finally could move on with her life.

Snapping her fingers, Loren knew what she needed to do. She had numerous phone calls to make. She needed to find a caterer, a reception hall, music, and a baker. And she needed to call her church. That one needed to be done first.

After countless phone calls, Loren was exhausted. She had set the date with the church, and gotten the music set up for the reception hall. But she needed Erik to go with her to talk about the food and to taste which kind of cake they would have.

She was excited. She was eager to tell Erik how much she had gotten accomplished and excited to begin a new life with him.

Just as she set the phone on the table, Jessie walked through the door. Loren was surprised to see her.

She glanced at the clock and couldn't believe how much time she spent making telephone calls. "Oh. I didn't even get dinner going. I've been talking all day to get the wedding stuff set up."

Jessie threw her purse on the couch and sat at the table with Loren. "You've gotten a lot done huh? Good for you. But I thought you would take the day to enjoy yourself though. You don't get too many days like this you know. And when Erik moves in, there will be even less. He'll have his hands all over you, all the time," she said and grinned.

"Ha-ha. I had some pampering time for me. I took a bath and had a nice breakfast. And I discovered it is really quiet in the house without you and Sammie. Quite honestly, I didn't like it. It was too much."

Jessie looked towards the living room. "Is that why "Sesame Street" is on?" she asked. She laughed and went to shut the television off.

Loren looked towards the living room and began to laugh herself. She'd been so absorbed in her phone calls that she hadn't even noticed.

Leaning against the counter, Jessie glanced at Loren's neck. She got an excited expression on her face. "You put the necklace on? I'm so proud of you. I didn't know if you would ever be able to do that. I know how hard it's been for you to have it laying around."

Loren felt the necklace hanging around her neck and smiled. "Yeah. I thought it was time. I thought it would be more . . . more moving when I put it on though. I guess I thought that Craig would be spiritually connected to it somehow. Or maybe I wanted him to be. But . . . it's just another necklace."

Jessie frowned. "It's not just another necklace and you know it. The sentimental value of it makes it priceless. It connects you and Craig in a way that I don't think that I'll be able to experience. What you two had was something beyond special. It was . . . it was magical. I loved to watch you two together. The way you talked and smiled, made me happy on the inside. It was like watching the best love story ever. And I got to see it in the flesh. It gives me hope that I'll find someone like that in this crazy world too. Obviously it wasn't with Derik."

"I don't know what to say. I didn't think anyone saw how we felt about one another."

"Are you crazy? Everyone did. You're a legend in this town. People will be talking about you and Craig for generations."

"Alright, now you're going too far."

"No really. People saw what you two had and talk about it. They still do. I've heard it with my own ears. And now you have the chance to have it all again with Erik. You're one lucky woman."

Loren smiled. She was proud of Craig and also of Erik. She knew Jessie was right. She was a lucky woman. "Thanks sis. I needed that."

Jessie sat down at the table and got a serious expression. "I have to tell you something though."

Loren's smile disappeared and she grew quiet. "What's wrong?"

"There's nothing wrong. I just wanted to tell you that I talked to my old landlord and I got my old apartment again."

"You what? Why?" Loren asked. She sat back in her chair stunned by her sister's news.

"You're going to be married pretty soon. You don't need me hanging around here."

"Jess, that's not for months. I don't want you to go. I want you here with me." She paused and thought for a moment. "Even after I get married you can stay here. There's enough room. I like you being here. Sam likes you being here. Don't go."

Jessie sighed. "Thank you Loren. It's good to feel needed and wanted. But it doesn't make sense to stay here until the day you get married. You need to get used to your big sister not being around. And, besides that, Sam needs to adjust too. Although, I think she'll have a harder time than you."

Loren scratched her head. "No really, we can make this work. We can. Maybe we can add on a suite off the house. Would you like that?"

"What's with you? You were fine before I got here. Why are you being like this now?"

"I don't know. I want to protect you, I guess. I don't want Derik to get a hold of you or anything else happen. I want you safe, with me."

"Um, if you remember, Derik got to me when I wasn't here. Both times. I didn't think you'd be like this. I'm sorry you feel this way, but I need to move on with my life just like you're moving on with yours. That's life Loren."

Loren stood up and walked over to the sink. She suddenly felt light headed and like she might throw up.

Jessie stepped behind her and rubbed her back. "Are you okay? What's going on with you?"

Suddenly, she needed to sit down. Sliding to the floor, Loren hugged her knees. 'I don't know. I just don't want you to leave."

Jessie sat on the floor beside her and continued rubbing her back. "Too much going on too fast?"

"I guess. I don't know."

"You're really sensitive right now."

Loren took in a big gasp of air. "I know." She began to cry.

Just then, Erik and Sam walked into the house. They were laughing and making funny faces at each other. When they saw Loren crying on the floor, their smiles disappeared.

Erik crunched down in front of her and grabbed her hands. "What's going on?"

Jessie touched Erik's hand. "It's me. I told her I got my old apartment and I'm going to move out."

Sam stomped her foot. "No. You can't Aunt Jessie. I like you being here."

Jessie stood up and gave Sam a hug. "Hey. Your mom and Erik are going to be married soon. You're going to have Sheena here too. There's not enough room for me in this house. You know I have a lot of stuff and I need a lot of room. Besides that, I have some furniture of my own that I would like to use."

Sam pulled away. "That's not fair," she hollered and ran up the stairs.

Jessie glanced at Loren and Erik, rolled her eyes, then she ran up the stairs to talk to Sam.

Erik sat down next to Loren. "Now, what's going on?"

Loren put her head on his shoulder. "I'm overwhelmed I guess. And now with Jessie leaving me . . ."

She saw Erik's muscles tighten. He put his arm around her shoulders and squeezed. He didn't say anything.

Loren whispered, "No response?"

Erik cleared his throat before he spoke. "I thought you were excited to move forward and have me move in here with you?"

"Yeah, I know. I'm still a little confused I guess," Loren said with a strained voice.

"Well, do you think you're making the right choice?"

"I don't know. Do you?"

"Of course I do. I'm here for you right now and always will be," Erik responded.

Loren lifted her head and turned to look at him. "I know you are. That's all I needed to hear. I'll be alright."

Erik hugged her and looked into her eyes. "Of course you will be. I just don't want you to get cold feet and leave me. When I say that I love you, I mean it. And I mean it forever."

"I love you too," Loren said and hugged Erik tight.

Chapter 23

*P*eeling potatoes for that night's supper, Loren decided it was a good time to talk to Sam. She watched as her daughter rinsed the potatoes and began to cut them into chunks on a cutting board. "Be careful. I don't want to go to the hospital before we get to eat."

Sam rolled her eyes and kept cutting the potatoes. "When are you going to stop treating me like I'm five?"

Loren giggled. "I don't think that will ever happen. You'll always be my little girl. Even when you have babies of your own, you'll still be my baby. That's how it goes when you're a mom. Your kids will always be your kids."

"Great. You're going to embarrass me when I'm older aren't you?"

"Maybe." Loren shook her head and put the pot of potatoes onto the stove. When she grabbed the salad to start preparing, she glanced at Sam and saw her twirl in a circle. "Are you getting your dance moves ready for the wedding? You are going to dance aren't you?"

Sam shook her hips and laughed. "Of course. And you have to dance with me. Can I invite Valerie to come?"

"I didn't think you would go without her. She can come to the rehearsal dinner too. I already figured she would." Loren paused. "Are you happy that Erik and I are getting married?"

Sam wrinkled her forehead and put her hand on her hip. "I told you he asked me and I said it was okay."

"I know you did. I just want to make sure that you are one hundred percent sure. I don't want to get married and you to not be happy."

"I like him mom. I think he's cool." She paused and looked like she was in deep thought. "I do have a question though. Do I have to call him dad after you get married?"

Loren giggled. "No. You can call him Erik or Mr. Fisher or whatever you want. He has no allusions that he's replacing your dad. If at some point you want to call him dad you can, but you need to know that you never have to."

"Thanks mom. Do I get to be the Maid of Honor?"

Loren smiled. "Don't you think Aunt Jessie's feelings would be hurt if I didn't ask her? I was thinking of having you as my junior bridesmaid."

Sam pouted. "That sounds babyish."

"Actually, it is a huge deal." She took Sam's hand and had her sit at the counter on a stool. "You already helped me find a dress, but you'll help with other decisions too. But the most important thing is that I . . . I want you to walk me down the aisle."

Sam's eyes got huge. "I'll walk you down the aisle? Isn't that your dad's job?"

"I don't know if they'll even make it for the wedding. I would hope they would, but when I talked to them they were in Europe and planned on staying there for a while. They didn't sound that excited to come here for another wedding."

Sam still looked astonished. "That's not very nice, but that's okay with me. This is so cool. I get to walk with my mom to get married. What else do I get to do?" she asked excitedly.

Loren smiled. "Well . . . after Erik and I give each other our vows, he would give you vows also."

"He'd give me vows? Why? I'm not marrying him."

Loren giggled. "Not marriage vows as husband and wife. He would give you vows that he would take care of you like a father. That he'll always be there for you like he'll be there for me."

Sam thought about it for a minute. "Huh. I didn't know they did stuff like that." She paused and thought some more. "I think that's cool." She jumped to the floor and raised her hands in the air. "I'll do it. I'll be your junior bridesmaid. I'm going to be the best junior bridesmaid ever!"

They hugged one another and danced around the room laughing. When they were both finally out of breath, they sat down and continued with the task of making dinner. Just as Sam began to mash the potatoes, Jessie walked into the house.

She plopped into a chair and exhaled loudly.

Loren sat in a chair beside her. "What's up sis?"

Jessie closed her eyes and shook her head. "You would never believe what happened today?"

Sam stepped from the kitchen and sat down next to Loren. She had a serious expression on her face. "What? What happened Aunt Jessie?"

"Derik. That's what happened. Derik," Jessie replied.

Loren took Jessie's hand into hers and glanced at her face and arms to make sure there were no bruises or cuts. "What did he do?"

Jessie exhaled loudly again and leaned back in her chair. "It was busy today. Man was it busy. I don't know why but . . . anyways, I was putting flowers in the cooler when I heard the bell ring above the door. Expecting another customer, I didn't look back but hollered that I'd be right there. They didn't say anything. Then I felt a hand rub me down my back. It gave me the chills. I turned around and . . . it was Derik." She stood up and shivered. She began to pace the floor. "I didn't know what to do. There wasn't anyone else in the store and my helpers had just left for the day. I was freaking out. But then I remembered I had my phone in my pocket. I went behind the counter to get space between us. He didn't say a word the whole time. He just stared at me. It freaked me out even more." Jessie sat back down and rubbed her hands together. "When he did talk it gave me the heebee jeebees. His voice was quiet and I could tell he was glancing around to make sure no one else was there. Then when I looked towards the door, I saw he had turned the deadbolt and locked it. I was scared."

Loren didn't know what to say or do. She was already frightened but happy that Jessie came home unharmed. She looked at Sam and saw fear in her eyes. "Maybe Sammie bear should go upstairs."

Sam looked at her and glared. "I can hear it mom. I'm not a little girl anymore."

"No . . . I think . . ."

Jessie interrupted. "She can hear. It's okay." She held Sam's hand and looked her in the eyes. "It is better she learns how men can be sometimes so she doesn't have the same thing happen to her." She looked towards Loren for approval and then continued her story. "Anyways, when he spoke it didn't even sound like him. He said 'I've missed you. I think you're making a mistake by leaving me. I'm the best thing that will ever happen to you. And that red haired man will never be anything.' I didn't know what to think. Then he started talking about us having a kid again. I stayed behind the counter but he started to edge towards me. Before he got back there, I dialed the police and left the phone on. I put it up on the counter so they could hear." Jessie paused and took a couple deep breaths. "He came around the counter and I couldn't get away fast enough. He grabbed me around the waist and licked my face. It was disgusting." She looked at Loren. "I thought he was going to . . . you know." She glanced towards Sam and tried to smile. "You okay Sammie?"

Sam nodded her head.

"Well, he grabbed me and I started to scream and kick at him. I hoped the cops were hearing it and were on their way. But I didn't know for sure so I had to try and save myself. When he turned his head a second, I grabbed a pair of scissors and scratched the hand he was holding me with. He let go and jumped back. He called me all kinds of names and started to throw flowers onto the floor." Jessie stopped talking. She walked into the kitchen to get a drink.

Loren went and turned the burners off on the stove so she could give Jessie the attention she deserved. She sat back at the table and waited for her to continue.

Jessie sat back down and took a long drink of her water. "I heard sirens down the street and I hoped they were for me. I ran towards the door. Right when I got there, Derik pulled my hair. I didn't care. I reached for the deadbolt and unlocked it just as he pulled me back. I don't think he noticed that it was unlocked. Just then, a cop came through the door with his gun pulled out." She started to laugh. "It was the same cop again who had arrested Derik two other times. What are the chances?"

Sam started laughing too. "That's funny. Derik's stupid."

"I guess you could say that," Jessie responded. "Anyways, the cop yells at Derik and he yells back at the cop. Then Derik says he only came here to tell me he's moving back to Nevada. He came to say goodbye. The cop says 'You have a funny way of saying goodbye'. I had a hard time not laughing. The cop looks at me and asks if I want to press charges. I just want Derik out of my life so I say to let him go and for him to get the hell out of town."

Loren was amazed. "You didn't press charges? He left town? He didn't hurt you? I don't know what to think."

Jessie laughed. "You don't know what to think? I don't either." She stared at her glass of water. "Do we have any beer? This isn't cutting it for me."

Loren went to the refrigerator and got Jessie a bottle of beer. When she sat back at the table, she still didn't know what to make of all of it. "When did he get out of jail? Did someone post bail for him? Will he have to come back for court?"

"I have no idea and I don't want to know." Jessie responded. "I just like the fact that he's leaving town. The cop said he would make sure he was gone and would watch for him in the future. He's a good guy. The cop that is.

"How are you going to know if he comes back to town or not? How do you really know he's leaving?" Loren asked.

"Gees, Loren. I don't know all the answers. I just know that the cop escorted him out of my store, had a talk with him, and then came back in to tell me that he'll watch for him in the future. That was it." She took a drink of her beer and then put her head on the table. "I guess I have to have faith that it will work out and that he'll stay gone. I mean, he has no house anymore since our lease ran out. Hell, I don't even know what happened with his clothes. I don't know if someone else went and got his stuff or not. I handed the landlord my key and haven't been back there since."

Sam, who had been sitting quietly, cleared her throat. She stared at Jessie and smiled. "You are the coolest person I know. You're tough, pretty, and wear awesome clothes. I want to be just like you when I grow up."

Jessie looked at her dumbfounded. "Thanks for the compliment but I think you have a hero other than me in this room." She looked at Loren and had tears in her eyes. "I think your mom is the coolest person ever. She has endured a lot more than me and still is loving and wonderful."

Loren didn't know what to say. She didn't know Jessie felt that way about her.

Sam looked at Loren then at Jessie and then back at Loren. "I think you're right. My mom is pretty cool," she said. She gave Loren a huge hug.

Jessie gave them each a hug and kiss. She finished her beer and went to get another one. She saw the food on the stove and sighed. "I didn't ruin dinner did I? It looks good."

Loren walked around the counter to the kitchen and gave Jessie a big squeeze. "You didn't ruin anything. You can help us finish if you're up to it."

Jessie smiled. "Of course I am. Just tell me what I need to do."

Chapter 24

*I*t was a beautiful day to stroll down the main street. Loren held Erik's hand in her hand and didn't want to let go. She liked how she felt loved and needed while being next to him. She smiled and looked up at Erik. He looked like he was content to be where he was too and that made Loren even happier.

They walked into the bakery shop and tried six different kinds of cake samples before they finally decided on a red velvet cake for their wedding. Then, after looking through numerous books, they agreed on a three tier cake with candy pearls and roses around it. It would also have a fountain with colored lights in the water, and strings of pearls cascading down. For the final touch, Loren found the right color of tangerine, which matched her dress, so they could have small roses incorporated into the cake with the same color.

When they left the shop, Erik gave Loren a big hug. "I never thought we would do something like that. I'm the happiest man ever. I'm finally on the way to marry the woman of my dreams."

Loren didn't respond. She was delighted too and pleased that Erik was so satisfied. It made her happy to make him happy. She hoped that she could feel the same for many years to come.

Looking around, Loren watched as the people moved down the street. Some of them seemed to be in a hurry to get to their destination, while others didn't look like they had a place to get to any time soon. There were moms pulling on their young one's hand to get them to stop reaching for a wrapper on the sidewalk or wanting to stop to look at a bug. There were men in business suits on their phones looking at their reflection in the windows to make sure their hair looked just right. And there were workers working in the middle of the street with people in their cars honking at them as they went by.

As she watched all of it, she felt like she and Erik were invisible. No one worried about what they were doing or waved to them from across the street. Everyone had their own agenda. So even with the streets being so busy, it felt like they had the town to themselves.

Loren looked down at Erik's hand holding hers and gleamed. His hand was so much bigger than hers and it made her feel safe. His strong hand made her feel like no one could break them apart. It made her feel like he would always be there to protect her.

But then, she remembered that she had thought the same of Craig. Although he kept her safe, he was still gone. She had thought he was strong too, like Superman. She thought he would never leave her or let anything come between their perfect relationship.

Then he had the accident and everything changed. It wasn't his fault, but her heart withered and her world became darker. She felt empty on the inside and slowly had to learn to not show it on the outside. She cried herself to sleep for months and had smelled his pillow until the smell of his shampoo and cologne had disappeared. She had become a different person.

"Are you okay? Your demeanor changed." Erik asked.

Loren took a deep breath and was mad at herself for ruining the moment. She didn't want it to happen every time she was feeling happier. "I'm sorry. I'm fine. It's a wonderful day and I'm glad we're together to enjoy it."

Erik gave her a confused look. "Okay. If you want to talk, you know I'm here for you."

"I know you are and I appreciate that. You're a wonderful man. I'm lucky that we found each other."

"I hope you know that. I think it was fate. I think it was time for both of us to start a relationship and fate thought we were perfect for each other."

Loren squeezed his hand and leaned on his shoulder. "I think you're right. It's been tough for me, but it's time for me to move on with my life. And having you makes it so much better. I mean that."

Erik sighed. "I love you Loren. I love you with all my heart and soul. I'm sure of it now that I wasn't meant to find another woman. I was meant to wait for you and Samantha. I couldn't ask for a better life than the one I have with you and plan on living for the rest of our lives." He inhaled and exhaled deeply. "I have to admit that it was pretty rough for me to go thirty some years without getting married or having a family. I had met a few nice women, but they don't come close to the way I feel about us. There's something about you that makes me crave more time with you. It's like you have an intoxicating aroma or personality that I can't get enough of. That I don't want to get enough of." He kissed the top of her head.

Loren wished she could give herself to him like he had given himself to her. She still couldn't escape the shame of knowing she was still in love with the memory of what she and Craig had. It always crept back into her mind and she ended up feeling guilt-ridden. Guilty for believing she was cheating on Craig somehow. She wondered if she would ever be free of those chains that held her emotions.

Trying to change her mood back to how it had been before the thoughts of Craig, Loren stopped and kissed Erik on the cheek. "I love you too. I'm delighted to have you in my, and Samantha's, lives. We are both blessed to have a man like you to take care of us and love us like you do. I'm trying really hard to move past some of the old way of thinking. I really am. But even if some of the old feelings still show up every once in a while, I still want to be with you."

They walked back to Erik's truck and he opened the door for her. As they drove back to Loren's house, Erik continued to hold her hand. He didn't let go until they had stopped and he put the truck into park.

As they entered the house, they were met by Sam. She was smiling sheepishly.

Loren took one look at her and put her hand on her hip. "What's going on Samantha? I know that look. What did you do?"

Sam continued smiling and leaned back and forth. "I know something that you don't."

Intrigued, Loren raised her eyebrows and got a mischievous smile on her face. "Really? What's that?"

Sam leaned toward her and put her hands around Loren's ear to whisper. "Aunt Jessie and Cody are boyfriend and girlfriend."

Loren smiled. "How do you know that? Were you spying on them?"

"No. I heard her talking on the phone to him. It was like 'I like you too' and 'I want to see you soon' and other stuff", Sam said and made funny faces while she spoke.

Erik laughed. "You shouldn't be listening to them. I'm sure she didn't want you eavesdropping on their conversation."

Sam leaned on the wall. "I wasn't trying to. I was just walking into the kitchen to get a snack. I can't help it if she didn't hear me when I went in there."

Loren snickered. "Yeah. I'm sure you made noises to make sure she knew you were there too, right?"

"I might have been a little too quiet. But isn't it cool. I like her having a boyfriend. I think Cody is a little weird, but I think he's nice too."

Jessie snuck up behind Sam while she was talking. "You were listening to my phone conversation?"

Sam jumped and then began to blush. "Oh. I . . . I didn't try to. I was getting a snack."

Loren and Erik laughed and headed towards the kitchen.

Loren looked back to see Jessie scolding Sam for listening to her and Cody. "I think Sam's in trouble with Jess for a while." She turned back to look at Erik. "What do . . ."

She was cut off when Erik put his hand around her waist and pulled her to him. He looked into her eyes and then kissed her with so much passion that Loren had to put her arms around his neck to keep from falling. Then just as fast he let her go.

Loren leaned against the refrigerator for support. "What was that for?"

"I want us to be married today. Do you want to fly to Vegas?"

"Where's this coming from? We have a date set and I have my dress. You can't wait a few more months?"

"No. No I can't. I want to be with you now. Watching you with Sam made me fall in love with you even more. I can't tell you why, but it did. I just love how I love you and how you're a good mom."

Loren didn't know what to say. Her mind whirled with the thought of flying to Vegas and wearing her dress there. But then their parents' wouldn't be there or any of their friends. What would she do about the deposits they already put down for the cake and caterer?

Erik hugged her tight. "Quit looking so worried. I guess I'll have to wait. You look frantic. I hope it was because you were thinking about the wedding plans and not thinking about being with me."

"No. I was thinking of all the planning I've done already. I told you that I want to be with you." Loren lifted her foot. "No cold feet here."

Erik hugged her tighter and wouldn't let go. "I don't want to lose you. I feel like I found the piece to the puzzle to make my life complete."

Loren pushed away and looked at him. "I'm not going anywhere." Then a thought popped into her mind. She grabbed his hand and began pulling him towards her bedroom.

"Now? With Sam and Jessie right there?" Erik asked.

Loren laughed. "Get your mind out of the gutter. I have something to show you."

Erik giggled. "Like I said. Now? With Sam and Jessie right there?"

Loren squeezed his hand and led him through the door of her bedroom. She sat him on the bed and stood in front of him. "You might find this dumb, but I wrote you a poem. Do you want to hear it?" she asked nervously.

Erik raised his eye brows. "A poem? For me? I've never had that done for me before. Of course I want to hear it."

Loren took a deep breath to calm her nerves and went to her dresser. There she dug down below her undergarments and pulled out a piece of notebook paper. She didn't know if she should stand in front of Erik like she was giving a speech or sit down next to him. Either way, she felt nervous and wished she wouldn't have told him about it. Shutting the dresser drawer, she decided to sit down beside him and then pushed the hair behind her ears.

Unfolding the paper, she noticed her hands were shaking and began to laugh. "This is ridiculous. I'm so nervous to read it to you." She handed him the paper. "Why don't you read it yourself?"

Erik smiled and handed the paper back to her. "No. You wrote it. You should read it."

Loren heard Jessie and Sam laughing from the kitchen. It seemed to make her even more nervous and she stood up to shut the door.

Taking another deep breath, she closed her eyes for a second. When she reopened them she glanced at Erik and saw him waiting patiently with a look of sincerity of his face. She sat back down beside him.

Taking yet another deep breath, Loren held up the paper and began to read it. She said, "Just by saying hello you brought us together. Now, I want to be with you forever. Just by saying hello you changed my life and soon I will become your wife. Just by saying hello you got my attention. Now we will have many adventures together, too many to mention. Just by saying hello, I soon fell in love. And for this, and you, I thank the Lord above. Thank you for saying hello because if you had not. I wouldn't know the love you have given me, and that's a lot."

Loren didn't move. She was waiting for Erik to start laughing or walk out of the room. But instead, she felt him turn and put his arms around her. When he pulled back and looked into her eyes, he had tears that were on the verge of falling.

He hugged her tightly. He said, "I've never heard something so wonderful in my life. You make me feel like the most loved man in the world. I could never make you feel the way you've made me feel right now. I will try, but I don't think I could ever top it." He wiped his eyes. "Loren, thank you. Thank you for making me feel so special."

K A Neemeyer

Chapter 25

Sitting in her office, Loren felt her eyes get heavy. She had been working on inventory sheets and order forms for hours. The shop had already been locked up hours ago and she was still working. It was times like these that she wished she was an employee instead of the boss. It would make her life a lot easier.

Rolling her shoulders and tilting her neck to try and get it to release some of the tension, she finally let out a groan. This day had gone on long enough. She wanted to be home with a cold drink in her hand, sitting in the living room, having a conversation with Jessie or Erik or even Sam. She didn't want to be here but still had more work to do.

Loren laid her head on her desk and closed her eyes. But even with her eyes shut she still saw the images of numbers and inventory sheets. She couldn't escape the work no matter what she did.

Feeling frustrated and tired, she decided to get herself a nice cup of coffee. When she went to the front room to pour herself a cup, she was startled by a knock on the front door of the store. She jumped and almost spilled the piping hot coffee all over. When she looked over, she saw Erik.

Loren smiled from ear to ear. He was a welcome sight. She ran to the door and turned the keys to let him in. When the door swung open, she threw herself into his arms and breathed him in.

"Wow. You're happy to see me huh?" Erik asked.

"I guess so. It's great to see you. What are you doing here?"

Erik gave her a kiss on the cheek and pushed her softly to get through the door so he could shut it. "Well, I called the house and Jessie said you had to work late. I wanted to make sure you didn't have a boyfriend in here or having a party without me. So I dropped everything, which was eating my dinner in front of the television, and came here."

"It's so good to see you. I get lonely in this place."

"Oh. So it's not me in particular. It's just you didn't want to be alone," he said jokingly.

Loren pushed him on the shoulder and laughed. "No. It's definitely you that I'm happy to see."

"Still no cold feet then?"

"Nope. I'm getting use to the idea of marrying you. I know it took a while but . . . I guess you'll do."

Erik took a step back and stared at her. "I'll do? Really? Could you go without this?" he asked. Then he pulled her to him. He kissed her gently at first but then with passion.

Loren closed her eyes and relished the kiss. She liked the taste of his mouth and how he held her so tightly.

Without trying to break their hold, she reached behind him and relocked the doors. Then she slowly began to walk backwards towards the back room. She really didn't want them being seen by people walking by. It was no one's business but theirs when it came to their private time.

Erik matched her steps and Loren felt like they had danced to the back of the store. They had been in perfect rhythm with each other as they took their methodical movements. It was something she would never forget. It was a new memory.

When they reached the back room, Erik pushed her up against a wall. He wasn't rough about it, but he did it hard enough to get her attention.

Loren heard herself gasp. She instantly had a desire to have him within her and liked the craziness of it being in her coffee shop. She pulled him closer to let him know she wanted more.

Erik obliged her with her request. He lifted one of her legs so she would wrap it around his thigh. He held on to it tightly with one hand and then kissed her with more desire and lust.

She felt her temperature rise. She swore someone turned on the heater from the warmth she was feeling. She wanted and needed to see how hot it could get.

Erik wouldn't break their connection. He continued to kiss her and finally lower his mouth onto her neck. There, he grazed her skin with his tongue until she had goose bumps.

Loren could feel him smile against her skin. She knew he liked how she reacted to him. She liked how she reacted to him too.

But he didn't stop there. He nibbled on the tip of her earlobe and then her shoulders. Then he moved back up to her mouth where he kissed her gently. He massaged her leg, which he was holding in his hand, and Loren liked the sensations of it.

Slowly, Erik let go of her leg and wrapped his hand around her arm. He pulled gently to lead her towards her office and Loren didn't have a problem with following him. When they reached the doorway, Erik looked around.

Letting her go momentarily, he went to her desk and began to remove the papers from it. He cleared her entire desk, without saying a word, before he took her by the hand. He led her to the desk and lifted her so she was sitting on the edge. Again, without saying a word, he lifted her shirt and threw it on the floor followed by her bra. Slowly and carefully, he lifted her hips off the desk so he could slip her shorts and panties from beneath her until she was sitting naked on her own desk.

Then, after he had her how he wanted her, he began to undress. He watched her face as he removed each piece of clothing from his buff body.

Loren thought she was going to go insane. She wanted to jump from the desk and have them both fall to the floor. However, she repressed her desires momentarily to let him lead their interaction.

She could feel her pulse begin to elevate and felt her heart beating fast in her chest. All the while, the man she loved, was undressing in front of her until he was as naked as she was.

Moving towards her, she saw he wanted her as much as she wanted him. When he was close enough to touch, she reached for him to be nearer.

Erik pulled away and took a step back and smiled. It was obvious that he wanted to be in control.

Slowly, he moved closer again and all Loren could do was wait impatiently. She watched as his muscles moved and his stomach tightened. She saw the hunger in his eyes and saw him lick his lips.

When he finally touched her skin with his hand, she thought she was going to explode. She hadn't had these feelings for so long and she wanted to satisfy every single one. She wanted Erik to satisfy them.

Finally, he was within inches of her and couldn't wait any more. He thrust into her and they both let out a moan of ecstasy.

Loren's head fell back towards the desk and she closed her eyes. She wanted to feel every movement until it was done.

They moved back and forth in perfect harmony. When Erik moved forward, Loren would move forward. When he moved back, she would move with him. It was sensual and erotic and Loren didn't know how much more she could endure without going crazy from the sensations.

For what seemed like hours, they touched, caressed, and satisfied each other until they both finally released with pure enjoyment. She stared at

Erik and couldn't believe how he had made her feel. She wanted to experience it again and again until the day she died.

After they got dressed and used the restroom, Erik carefully put everything back on the desk where he had found it. Then, he pulled her to him again and kissed her sensually. Finally, he pulled away and stared into her eyes. "So . . . are you still settling for me?" he asked teasingly.

Loren sat in her chair and folded her arms in front of her. She smiled. "I guess I'll have to think about it."

Erik laughed. "You would have to think about it, wouldn't you? Now what?"

She stared at the papers on her desk. She knew she definitely wouldn't be able to concentrate on them now. The mood to work was completely gone. "I guess I lock up and leave. How about you?"

"Well, instead of me eating the frozen dinner I had warmed up earlier, I thought we could go for a bite to eat. That is why I came over here. You made the circumstances different."

Loren grinned. "Oh . . . that was my fault. I see. And yes, I'd like some dinner."

"Great. Sheena ate my dinner before I left anyways. Where are you taking me then?"

"I don't know. What are you hungry for?"

"I'm plenty satisfied," Erik responded.

She laughed. "I'm talking food you naughty man."

"Oh. Then how about some pizza?" Erik asked.

Loren took his hand and they headed out the door. "Sounds good to me."

They strolled down the block to the local pizzeria, ordered a pizza and drinks, and then sat down across from one another. Loren looked around to see college age kids at almost every table. "I feel old in here."

Erik glanced around and smiled. "Nah. We're just a little older. Not by much though. They could learn from us."

Loren giggled and liked how Erik ended up making every situation feel good in the end. She loved his smiled and couldn't believe that, not even an hour ago, they had been entwined in sweet desire. Now they sat in a restaurant and were going to eat pizza.

Loren admired the décor of the restaurant. She noticed they had gone with the sports theme and had every sport imaginable portrayed on the walls. From golf to wrestling and from football to soccer. It was all there.

When she glanced around, she could see numerous jerseys and napkins with autographs that were put behind glass to protect them. She wondered how long it had taken to get so many signatures or if they bought them off the internet.

Smelling a pizza being brought to another table made Loren's stomach grumble. The aroma made her realize she hadn't eaten since breakfast and it was now eight o'clock at night. Wanting some of the food, she watched as the pizza was placed at a table with a group of young men. They each grabbed a large slice and stuffed large bites into their mouths. Loren grinned as she watched them hardly swallow a chunk of food before they shoveled another bite into their mouth.

Directing her attention back towards Erik, she looked at his features. In the time they had known each other, he seemed to get more handsome every time she saw him. Smiling to herself, she figured he would be one of those guys that would get better looking with age while she turned gray and wrinkly.

The thought of growing old together and seeing how they would be, made Loren happy on the inside. She knew this was good for them to be together. It felt right to be with him so much of the time. She just needed to learn how to drown out the feelings the other times when she thought of Craig. She needed to realize that she wasn't cheating on him or hurting him in any way. It wasn't possible to do that. He wasn't with her.

Lost in her thoughts, she didn't hear the waitress when she asked her to move her arm so she could put the pizza on the table. Erik tapped on her shoulder and pointed to the pizza. "Oh. I'm sorry. That looks delicious."

Along with the food, the waitress brought them each a tall glass of beer. Loren began to salivate just thinking of the flavors combined. She didn't even wait for the plates to set on the table before she grabbed a slice of pizza.

Erik laughed. "A little hungry tonight?"

Loren smiled as she chewed. She liked the taste of the sauce, cheese and meat on her tongue. She didn't want the flavors to ever disappear. So with that, she took another bite to enjoy the flavors again. When she was done chewing, she wiped her mouth and grinned. "Yes. I'm starving. I wasn't expecting to work late tonight so I didn't bring anything to eat. I figured I would hurry and get done and go home for some dinner. But then I forgot about the inventory stuff and it was taking longer than I thought it would. Then . . ." she smirked at Erik. "Then I had some company and didn't get my work done anyways." She took a big drink and took another bite of her food.

Erik stared at her. "I thought it all ended up going pretty good. It wasn't what I had intended, but I'm not complaining. Not one little bit. I'm actually pretty damn happy that I went to visit you."

"Me too. It was a welcome break and treat. The only bad thing is that I'm gonna have to get up early in the morning to finish it all. I have to get it done tomorrow for sure."

"Why's that?" Erik asked curiously.

Loren sighed. "Let's just say that I'm gonna need a day off."

Erik tilted his head and looked confused. He wrinkled his forehead then he frowned. "Oh. I know why. Just don't forget that I'm always here for you. Call me if you need me. Okay?"

"Of course. I know you are and I know I can count on you to keep your word." She touched his hand. "I love you Erik Fisher. I love you very much."

K A Neemeyer

Chapter 26

As soon as Loren opened her eyes, she knew it wasn't going to be a good day. Although she had tried to make it a pleasant day in the past. It never worked. She had accepted it for how it was and tried to handle it the best she could.

It was the anniversary of Craig's death. It was the day the emotions would take over and Loren didn't know how to stop them from happening. It was the day she always would remember as the worst, heart wrenching, and saddest day of her life.

Loren turned on her side and thought maybe she would stay in her bed for as long as possible. She didn't want to start the day or relive the memories again. No. She only wanted to escape the bad feelings and try and focus on the good.

Outside her door, she could hear footsteps pacing on the wood floor. Loren shook her head and rolled her eyes. She knew the idea of staying in bed was not going to happen as she wanted.

Dragging herself from under the covers and putting on a robe, she opened the door and saw her daughter. Sam had tears in her eyes. When Loren looked closer, she thought she looked like she hadn't slept all night.

"What's wrong Sam?" Loren put her arms around her and squeezed. "Never mind. I know what's wrong. But why do you look so tired?"

Sam leaned against Loren and cried. "I thought I'd try and stay up all night so that I could sleep all day today. I thought I could do it, but I fell asleep. Now I have to be awake. I don't want to be awake mommy. I want to sleep and not be awake today."

Loren sighed. "I know. I know." She put her hand under Sam's chin and lifted her face to look at her. "I thought of doing the same thing. But we have each other to get through the day. Okay?"

"Okay."

They both crawled into Loren's bed and covered their heads with the blankets.

Loren listened to Sam's breathing and it helped her to relax. "I love you Sammie bear. I wish this day would get easier and I'm sure that someday it will. Is there something you want to do to take your mind off of it?"

Sam pushed the covers off their heads and stared at the ceiling. "I don't know. I would like to play with Valerie but I don't think I'd have fun." She looked at Loren with a serious expression. "Daddy likes it that we think of him today, doesn't he?"

Loren smiled. "Sweetie, we think of him every day. It's just that today is harder to bare. It makes us think of the bad instead of the good. So let's really try to think of the good things about your daddy today okay?" Loren tried to think. "I know. How about we make him a card. We'll make it ourselves and bring it to him. What do you think?"

Sam smiled. "I think that's a great idea." She pushed the covers off of her, sat up, and dangled her feet off the side of the bed. She looked back at Loren with sparkles in her eyes. "I think he'd like that. I'm going to make the best card ever." She jumped off the bed and headed out of the room. "I'll meet you in the dining room. I'm gonna get dressed and get some paper and stuff."

Loren watched her run from the room. She leaned on her elbow and glanced down at the necklace dangling from her neck. She grasped the heart in her hand and stared at the diamonds before she fell back onto her pillow. She had tears in her eyes, but she smiled. "I miss you Craig. I miss you with all my being. I miss the way you looked, the way you smiled, and how you made me feel so loved. I miss everything about you."

Sitting up she let the heart from the necklace fall back to her chest. She knew this day was going to be hard but she had to get through it. Besides, staying in bed wasn't going to be an option.

Loren got dressed and put her hair back into a pony tail. She slipped on her shoes before she headed into the dining room. When she looked at the table, she saw Sam working intently.

Loren smiled and went into the kitchen to make some coffee.

Just then, she saw Jessie walk into the room and sit next to Sam. "What are you doing?"

Sam spoke softly but didn't look up. "I'm making daddy a card. Mom and I are going to bring it to him today."

Jessie looked over at Loren with a sad face. "Oh. I forgot." She walked into the kitchen and gave her a hug. "How are you doing?"

Loren smiled. "I'm okay. Sam and I are doing something special and then go see Craig in a while. You can come if you want."

Jessie frowned. "I have to work today. I'm sorry. I'll be home later." She gave Loren a kiss on the cheek and headed for the door. Before she stepped out, she looked back at Loren. "Tell Craig hello from me. I miss that guy."

Loren watched Jessie drive away and then got Sam and herself a muffin. She sat at the table with her daughter and nibbled on her breakfast as she helped cut out some hearts. Then she glued them on to the pink paper Sam had chosen. They cut out more hearts and letters to make the perfect card. When they were done they both looked at it with pride.

The card was cut in to a large heart with smaller hearts glued sporadically around it. Sam had wanted letters to spell out "I love you" to put in the center. Finally, she added some glitter and signed her name with a black marker.

Sam gleamed. "I think he'll love it."

Loren patted her on the back. "I think you did a wonderful job." She took in deep breath and exhaled. "Are you ready to go give it to him?"

Sam's smiled disappeared. "I guess so." She stared at the card. "Mom? Do you think you could take the card yourself? I don't want to go. It's too hard."

Loren closed her eyes and wished she could take any pain Sam felt away from her. "I can do that. I can call Jodelle and see if Valerie wants to play."

Sam sighed. "Can I just stay home myself? I don't really feel like playing today."

"Stay home yourself? You've never done that. Are you sure that you're comfortable with that?" Loren asked.

She looked into Loren's eyes. "Mom. I'm ten years old. I think I can handle being home by myself for a while. Please? I don't want to have my heart hurt like it always does when I go there." She folded her hands on the table and looked at Loren with sincerity.

Loren thought for a few seconds before she answered. She tilted her head to one side and smiled. "You are growing up, aren't you? Some days I don't think that I like it too much."

Sam stood up and gave Loren a hug. "I know. But you can't stop it. Even if you put a brick on my head."

Loren giggled. "Hey. That's my line." She admired the card they created and then grinned at Sam. "Yes. I'll take your beautiful card to your dad." She paused. "I guess I'll be back in about a half hour or so. I'll have my phone if you need to call me. You'll call me if you need me, right?"

"Yes mom. I'm gonna go to my room and listen to music and look through my photo album of dad and me. I'll see you in a little while."

Loren watched Sam skip up the stairs and disappear through her bedroom door. She shook her head and tried to grasp the idea of leaving her baby girl home alone. It was a hard day already without thinking of Sam growing so fast.

Grabbing a cup of coffee on her way out, Loren yelled up the stairs to say she was leaving. After hearing Sam yell goodbye, she headed out the door. Once she sat herself in front of the steering wheel, Loren stared at the house. She glanced up at Sam's bedroom window to see if she would wave. Not seeing the curtains move, Loren sighed and started the engine.

As she headed towards the cemetery, she thought about all the changes in her life. It all seemed to happen so fast with Jessie moving in and deciding to move back out, Sammie growing up faster than Loren wanted, and Erik giving her a ring. Everything seemed to be changing except for the way she felt about Craig being gone.

Loren parked at the gate of the cemetery and walked towards Craig's head stone. She tried to concentrate where she was walking so she didn't trip on the holes that little ground animals had dug to hide or find food. It bothered her that they didn't know what this place was and to stay away. But they didn't know, so she just had to accept the ways of nature.

As she stepped in front of the tombstone with the double hearts with Craig's name on the left heart, she took a deep breath to calm her nerves. Every time she came here, she felt overcome from the pain of her broken heart. But she pushed through the feelings and knelt down to place the card Sam had made. She looked around for a small stone or branch to keep it from blowing away. Then she cursed to herself for not thinking of bringing something along with her to keep the card in place.

After finding a long branch, she broke off a chunk to put on top of the card. She placed it and the branch gently on the ground in front of Craig's gravestone. She stared at it for a few minutes while a soft breeze moved the edges and glitter blew into the air.

Shaking her head, Loren sat on her behind and crossed her legs. She touched the stone and felt the smoothness of it. "Hello there Craig." Loren leaned her head back to look at the sky for a moment before she continued speaking. "Well, it's that day again. And well . . . I still don't know how to deal with it. I still don't know how to handle not having you with me. I'm trying. I really am. I'm trying to move on with my life but it's so damn hard." She looked at her engagement ring and tears filled her eyes. When she looked back at the tombstone, the letters of Craig's name were blurry. She wiped her eyes and stared at his name again. Suddenly, she began to feel angry. Her voice got louder. "You weren't supposed to leave me. You were supposed to be with me until we were old and Sam took over the house. Do you remember that? We talked about it. But now you left me here alone."

Loren tried to get control of her emotions. She thought she would feel sad today. But instead, she was angry. This was all new to her. She had never felt angry at Craig for leaving. It wasn't his fault.

Looking around the cemetery, she figured no one was ready for their love one to be gone. She couldn't imagine all the tears that had fallen on these grounds.

She looked back at Sam's card and smiled. "Your little girl made this card for you. She didn't come with me today though. She's growing up so fast. I hope you can see what a wonderful young woman she's becoming." She paused. "I wish I didn't have to leave her home alone so I could come visit her father in a graveyard."

Loren fidgeted with the ring on her finger. "Did I tell you that Erik asked me to marry him? He gave me a ring now. It feels weird to have another ring on. I never thought I would. I have our wedding rings in a safety deposit box for Sam to have when she's older." She closed her eyes. "That's wrong. It's wrong to have our rings tucked away for a rainy day. Why? Why did you leave me? I feel like I'm being forced to remarry and move on with my life." She looked at her ring and thought of Erik's loving smile.

307

"No. . . . I'm not being forced. Erik's a good man. He loves me and Sam. . . . But he made the same promises as you. To be with me forever. To take care of us. How can I believe him? I had believed you and look where I'm sitting."

Loren had tears running down her cheeks. She felt them fall onto her arms but ignored it. She couldn't concentrate on anything but the pain. The pain of Craig being gone and leaving her to make so many choices on her own.

Again, she felt mad. She was angry but not at Craig. She was angry for him being taken from her. She was angry for the love she would miss from him. She was mad because she didn't get to say good bye or give him one last kiss. Her emotions were overwhelming.

She hugged her knees with her arms to try and get control of herself. She had to calm down so she could get back home to Sam. She needed to get back home to Sam.

Loren wiped her eyes. She slowly got up to her knees and then her feet. Looking down at the card one last time, her heart seemed to weigh a hundred pounds itself. "Sam couldn't come today because it hurts her too much. It hurts me too, but I need to be here. I will come here until the day I die and am lying beside you." Loren suddenly felt nauseous. She thought of Erik and being married to him. "Oh no. When I die . . . do I lay beside you . . . or Erik?"

K A Neemeyer

Chapter 27

*J*essie and Loren began to pack Jessie's belongings into the same boxes they had been packed in before. Sam watched them work while she had her arms folded and a hurt look on her face.

Jessie glanced up at Sam from the closet. "I'm sorry you don't want me to go. But you have to understand that it's time. I need to run my own life."

Loren patted Sam on the knee and smiled. "She's right. She needs to live on her own time. She shouldn't have to worry about fixing dinner for us or sharing a bathroom. She's a little old for that. Although I must say that I love her staying here as much as you do."

Jessie threw a hand full of shoes into a box and pushed the hair from her face. She smiled at Sam and pointed towards the closet. "Did you want to pick out a few things to keep for yourself? And then you can come and stay at my place for the night and we can trade the clothes you borrowed for some new ones. What do you think of that?"

Sam's eyes got wide and she smiled. "You'd let me do that? I mean, Aunt Jessie, you'd let me borrow some of your stuff? That would be so cool."

Jessie laughed. "Oh, now I see why you didn't want me to leave. It's not for me, it's for my clothes."

Sam put her hands in front of her and waved them. "No. I don't want you to go at all." She thought for a moment and smiled. "It's just that you have such cool clothes and . . . well, I want to wear them."

Loren and Jessie both laughed.

Loren patted Jessie on the shoulder and looked back at Sam as she left the room. "Don't take too many of her clothes. We don't want her to be going around the town naked."

"Ah mom! Stop it."

Loren laughed at herself and headed down the stairs. She needed to get them some lunch before they started moving boxes to Jessie's apartment. When she reached the bottom of the stairs, she heard her phone ring and ran across the kitchen to answer it.

"Is this Loren Quinn?"

"Yes. Who am I speaking with?"

"Hello sweetie. This is Georgia, from Erik's office."

Loren got an uneasy feeling. This was the first time Georgia had ever called her before. "What can I do for you Georgia? Is everything alright?"

"Well . . . no. I hate to be the one to tell you this, but . . . Erik was in a car accident."

Loren heard a ringing in her ears and her hands began to shake. "What?"

"It just happened. They couldn't find his phone, but they saw his business card so they called me. I don't know how bad it was. I figured I should call you first so you could get to the hospital," Georgia said softly.

"I can't do this again."

"I don't understand," Georgia whispered and sounded confused.

Loren leaned against the kitchen counter and tried to get a hold of her emotions. She couldn't help but to feel like she was talking to the nurse that told her that Craig had been in an accident. Her legs become numb and tears slid down her cheeks. "I can't lose him too. I don't know if I can do it again. I . . ."

Georgia sighed. "Loren, you'll be okay. You need to take a deep breath and try to relax. Like I said, I don't know how bad it is. It could be nothing. Just calm down. Do you want me to come pick you up? Just give me your address and I can come get you."

Loren felt dizzy and sat down at the table. She thought she might throw up but fought back the urge. "No. My sister is here. She can take me. Thank you."

Loren hung up the phone and began to cry uncontrollably. She couldn't stop.

Her thoughts went to Craig and how she was too late to say good-bye. Images of being by his bedside with his blood smeared on the sheets plagued her mind. She could hear herself screaming as she looked at his lifeless face. The same face she had just kissed earlier that dreadful morning.

The same emotions of feeling instantly lost without him and not knowing how to react began to take over. It felt like a hand had grasped her heart and squeezed. She felt like she couldn't breathe. She tried to take a deep breath and it hurt. She couldn't focus. Everything became blurry.

Loren took a few smaller breathes to try and get control. But she still had a hard time filling her lungs with air. She was frantic. She didn't know if she could go through it all again. What if the same thing happened to Erik? What if he was laying lifeless in a bed and she would have to see him that way?

She knew she needed to get up to get to the hospital. If he was badly hurt, she wanted the chance to say good-bye this time. She needed to do that for her own sanity.

She tried to stand up but her legs wouldn't move. She tried to holler for Jessie but no sound would come out. Not knowing what else to do, she called Jessie's cell phone and heard it ring upstairs.

"Hello? Why are you calling me Loren? Aren't you downstairs?"

Loren couldn't speak. She was in shock.

Jessie laughed and hung up the phone.

Loren dialed her number again and heard it ring again.

"Loren. This is stupid. Why are you calling me?"

Loren held the phone close to her mouth. She heard her voice tremble when she spoke. "I need you."

Loren heard heavy footsteps upstairs and then heard Jessie run down the stairs. She hollered Loren's name twice before she saw her at the table.

Jessie fell onto her knees and grabbed Loren's hands. She had a worried look on her face and spoke softly. "What's wrong? You were only down here for a second. What's wrong? Are you hurt?"

Loren tried to talk between hiccups from crying. "Erik. He . . . he was in an accident."

"Oh no!" Jessie yelled. "How? Where? How do you know?" she asked frantically.

Loren squeezed Jessie's hands in hers. She closed her eyes and took a deep breath. "His secretary called. He's been in a car accident. We need to get to the hospital." Loren looked at Jessie with a look of terror. "What if it's the same thing as Craig? What if he left me too? What if I'm already too late?"

"Stop it. Stop it now. He's not Craig. Now let's go so we can find out what happened. It could just be a little fender bender and they brought him to the hospital to make sure he didn't have whiplash or something. Now, get up and let's go," Jessie said as she pulled on Loren's hands to get her to her feet.

Loren felt like she had been drugged. Her ears sounded like they were plugged and that her legs had twenty pound weights attached to each of them. She could still hear Jessie call Sam downstairs but it sounded mumbled, like they were far away. Then she felt Jessie pull on her arm and practically dragged her to the SUV. She heard Sam asking questions and could see Jessie look towards her with a look of concern. They drove for miles without anyone saying a word. Then she felt Sam tap on her shoulder and Loren jumped in her seat. "What Sam?" Loren asked sharply.

Sam sat back in her seat. "Sorry. I was just asking if you knew what happened to Erik."

Loren heaved a sigh. She turned so she could look back at Sam. "Sorry baby. I don't know. I just know that he's hurt, but I don't know how bad it is. I guess we'll find out when we get there."

Sam looked out the window. When she looked back at Loren, she had tears in her eyes. "He's not going to die, is he?"

Loren's heart ached. "I don't think so, but I can't tell you he's fine either, because I don't know what happened. Let's just pray that he's alright."

Sam looked back out the window and Loren turned her direction towards Jessie. When Loren looked at her, she could see the worry on her face. She put her hand on Jessie's shoulder and tried to smile. "Thanks for being there for me again. I'm glad you didn't move out yet. I don't know what I would have done." She paused. "Sam can't drive yet," she said trying to make a joke.

Jessie didn't smile or take her eyes off the road. When she spoke, it sounded quiet and concerned. "You need to be ready for anything. It could be something small or something . . . you just need to be ready. You have to be strong for Sam. Last time you fell apart, but Sam was still little. This time she's older and needs you more."

Loren glanced back at Sam to make sure she wasn't listening. "I know. Just get there so we can find out."

Jessie pulled into the visitors' area of the hospital. Quickly, they all pushed through the front door and walked up to the front desk. There, Loren asked for any information about Erik and the nurse gave her a concerned look.

"Are you family?" the nurse asked.

Loren got an uneasy feeling that they wouldn't let them back to see him. "No. I'm his fiancé. I got a call from his secretary at his office. Can you please tell me what's going on?"

The nurse typed on her keyboard and stared at the monitor. She frowned for a moment and then typed some more. Finally, she pointed towards the monitor and looked up at Loren. "Are you Loren Quinn?"

"Yes I am," Loren answered.

The nurse smiled. "Okay. He has you on the list of approved visitors." She smiled again. "He actually had you put on the list months ago when he came in for some routine blood work."

Loren's heart beat hard in her chest. She wanted to see him more than she ever had before. "His room number please."

The nurse frowned. "I'm sorry. It looks like he's in surgery right now. You'll have to be seated and I'll be sure to make a note so the doctor comes out to talk to you.

Jessie looked shocked. "Surgery? For what? How serious was the accident?"

"I don't know any more then that he's in surgery. Sorry." The nurse seemed frustrated with not being able to tell them more. "I'm sure someone will be out soon to talk to you." She pointed towards the waiting area. "There's coffee and a vending machine down the hall. Please make yourself as comfortable as you can." She looked at Sam and smiled at her. "There is a computer with games on it if you're interested."

Sam grabbed Loren's hand and smiled back at the nurse. "Thank you, but I'll sit with my mom."

The nurse looked back at her computer and they turned to take a seat among the rows of chairs lined up against the walls and in the center of the room. Loren looked around and had a shiver go down her back.

The room had warm colors, but it still seemed hard and unfriendly. The pictures were of abstract art that looked more like ink blots than art to Loren. The florescent lights gave the room the impression of being in an office instead of a place to try and relax while the rows of chairs made Loren feel like she was waiting to have her taxes done. Although there were a few large plants, none of them helped her become more at ease or wanting to sit there for a long period of time.

She sat in one of the plastic chairs and Sam sat on one side of her and Jessie on the other. Sam looked like she was ready to cry and Loren held her hand to try and reassure her it would be alright even if she didn't think it herself.

Jessie fumbled through her purse and reached for some gum. She offered them each a piece and then sat next to Sam to have her look at her phone. They began to look at websites with shoes and boots and Loren was grateful that Jessie was trying to take Sam's mind off where they were.

They had only been sitting there a couple minutes before Loren was already feeling claustrophobic. She wanted to go home or go outside into the fresh air, but knew that wasn't possible. So instead, she stood up and walked around to try and push the feelings away.

Looking at the artwork, she tried to concentrate on its design but couldn't figure out what it was supposed to be and figured that's how the artist intended it. Not wanting to try and focus on it anymore, she went to get a cup of coffee but decided against it just as she was going to pour herself a cup. When that didn't work at calming her nerves, she saw a pile of magazines and thought she could search through them but couldn't find anything that interested her. After that she walked to the vending machine and looked to see if there was anything there that she might want. There wasn't. Finally, she stared out the window, but it made her want to leave even more, so she went and sat back down.

Loren tapped her foot on the floor and pushed the hair from her face. She watched Jessie and Sam look for the perfect pair of shoes and wished they would converse with her instead. She didn't know what to do. She felt like she was going to go insane. She wanted to run, scream, and pull her hair at the same time. She wanted to kick the chairs and tear the artwork off the walls. She wanted to see the coffee stain the floor after she threw the pot down as hard as she could. She needed to know what was happening with Erik before she went completely mad.

At long last, after an hour of waiting, a female doctor with short brown hair and big blue eyes came through the door and looked around the room. When she looked towards Loren, she had a troubled look on her face. She stood in front of them and spoke to all three. "Hello. I'm Dr. Young. I'm assuming that you're here for Erik Fisher?" When they all nodded, she continued. "Well, let me start by telling you that he is going to recover just fine. He had quite the accident, but he was wearing his seatbelt and the airbags also helped. He did have his leg broken from the impact from the truck that hit him."

Loren felt the color drain from her face. She couldn't believe what she was hearing. She had so many questions and needed them answered. "A truck? Like a semi-truck?"

Dr. Young nodded. "He was very lucky. If the truck would have hit him from a different direction, it could be a lot worse. He's banged up a bit, but he's going to recover from it." She took a breath and gathered her thoughts. "He has a broken tibia and we had to insert a metal rod and screws to align it correctly. It will take . . ."

Loren didn't hear much more. She heard three to six month recovery, staples, and crutches. She couldn't concentrate on what the doctor was saying. She just wanted to go and see that Erik was alright for herself. She needed to know that he could look at her and smile. She needed to know that he was still with her and wasn't going to leave her. She needed to know that he was still alive.

"Okay? Any questions you have for me?" the doctor asked.

Loren tried to concentrate on the doctor's face. She looked young and couldn't have been a resident doctor for too long. "I'm sorry. I didn't catch everything that you said. I . . ."

Dr. Young interrupted. "It's alright. It's a lot to take in right away. You can go see him now. I'll walk you to his room. I can explain it all again later." She pointed them in the right direction and waited until they were following her. She glanced back over her shoulder and spoke with a soft tone. "Now please understand that he did just wake up from the anesthesia and might be groggy. But he'll be talking in no time at all."

K A Neemeyer

Chapter 28

*L*oren needed to take a walk. She had so many built up emotions and needed a release. She started to think that she was going crazy.

When she went to leave Erik's room, she saw Jessie give her a concerned look.

Jessie followed her out the door and grabbed her arm. "Are you okay? Erik looks pretty good considering what happened. All the bruises and scratches will be gone before you know it. Of course his leg will take longer to heal but . . . it should be healed before the wedding."

Loren gave her hug and didn't want to let go. "I think I'm fine. I just have a lot of feelings to work through."

Jessie pulled her away and looked into her eyes. "Are you okay?"

Sighing, Loren held her hands. "I'm fine. Erik doesn't look too bad. I'm happy for that. It's just . . ."

"It's just what? I don't understand Loren. Aren't you happy that he's okay?"

Loren furrowed her eyebrows. "Of course I am. I can't believe you would ask something like that. He means so much to me. If he didn't, I wouldn't have went and bought a wedding dress." She inhaled a big breath and blew it back out. "It was just all the emotions leading up to finally seeing him. I couldn't help but to think of Craig. I just wish that . . . that I could have seen him alive too. I just wish . . ."

Jessie hugged Loren close. "I know. I know. I wish you could have too. But you have Erik in front of you now and he needs you. He loves you and wants you beside him through this. Maybe it's a good idea for you to take a walk and get your head on straight." Jessie pulled back and looked at Loren. "Don't forget about what you have right in front of you. Don't lose that."

Loren gave Jessie another hug and headed down the hallway. She headed out a side door and followed the sidewalk not knowing where it led. As she walked around the corner of the hospital, she saw a small flower garden with a water fountain in the middle of it. Loren was surprised. She hadn't known it even existed. Even so, she thought it looked beautiful and admired the flowers that were blooming as she walked.

As she got closer, she noticed the beauty of the water fountain. It was a warm beige marble with three tiers. Each tier got smaller the higher it was displayed. As she studied the design, she thought each one reminded her of a large scallop seashell holding as much water as it could until it spilled over the edges.

In the middle of the fountain, there were two dramatic angels. They each had large elaborate wings that rested on the angel's back. One angel was sitting with his feet crossed in front of him and looked to be deep in thought while the other had his hands raised and looked towards the heavens. Loren admired the beautiful artwork and let the sound of the water begin to drown out her thoughts. Already feeling more at ease, she sat down on the edge of the big fountain and let the noises of the water soothe her mind.

She had always liked water. Since she was little she would love to take baths and have the water running while she played. She had enjoyed the swimming pool, mostly because of the sounds of kids splashing, and the feel of the cool water too. She always seemed to be attracted to the splashing of water and as her thoughts melted away she knew why.

Loren closed her eyes and tried to envision herself sitting on a beach on a large beach towel. She imagined her skin was warm and she had to shield her eyes from the sun's rays. And as the sun shined down on her, she was comfortable and at peace.

Deep in thought, she heard herself moan. Loren quickly opened her eyes and looked around to make sure no one was watching or listening to her. Suddenly, she felt embarrassed and walked away from the water fountain. But the further she walked from it, the louder her thoughts became again.

As she headed towards a bench that was wrapped around a tree, she tried to hold back the tears that wanted to slip down her face. She didn't want to cry anymore. She didn't want to hurt, or worry, or think of the worst. She needed to concentrate on what was good. But when she thought of Erik lying in the hospital bed, she couldn't think of anything pleasant.

She believed she was being tortured from the emotions of her past mixed with the new emotions now. But she couldn't seem to get past the thoughts of Craig or the sensations she had experienced then. And now, with Erik being in a car accident too, she didn't know how to handle it all. The feelings were now layered on top of each other and she had more to get through.

Loren sat down on the bench and leaned back so her head was on the tree. She looked up into the branches and watched the leaves dance with the wind. In the distance, she could still hear the faint sound of the water from the fountain. If she really concentrated, it looked like the leaves were dancing to the rhythm of the water.

Absorbed by the sounds of the water and leaves above her, Loren momentarily forgot where she was. She didn't feel claustrophobic and her thoughts became calmer. The ideas of hospitals and surgeries and pain disappeared.

When she finally lowered her head, Loren didn't know how long she had been staring into the tree. It had felt like hours. Nonetheless, when she looked at her phone and saw it had only been a few minutes, she was sad. She had wanted it to be longer, but to have some peace was good enough for now.

Loren looked at the hospital exterior and thought it looked cold compared to the warmth she felt from being in the small gardens. It amazed her how a fountain and a tree could make her feel so much more alive. She didn't want to go back into the hospital and feel the dreariness again. She wanted to remain here.

But then she thought of Erik in the hospital bed with a broken leg. Her thoughts were instantly corrupted and the beauty of the park disappeared. The leaves on the tree might as well have shriveled and fallen to the ground along with the fountain freezing or ceasing to work. Her thinking became darker and unkind. Her thoughts went back to the death of her first love and she couldn't escape them.

Tears began to fall from her eyes. She thought of Craig and the agony he must have endured. The thought of him yelling for her and her not knowing he was even hurt was almost impossible to bear. Then she thought of him saying her name as he took his last breath and she believed her heart was going to rupture from the pain.

She didn't know how to say sorry to him for her not being there when he needed her most. She couldn't. He was gone.

Loren looked back up at the tree and a ray of sunlight shone through the leaves and penetrated her face. She could feel its warmth and it instantly gave her a new sense of hope. It made her remember that Erik was still with her. He needed her. And while she couldn't be there for Craig, she could be there for Erik. She needed to be there for him.

She needed to forgive herself for not being there for Craig. It was better she hadn't been there and witnessed the pain he went through. That would have traumatized her more. And although she didn't get to say good-bye, she needed to realize that it wasn't her fault and to forgive herself. She knew in her heart that Craig didn't hold a grudge against her and she needed to stop holding one against herself. She needed to free herself from her past so she could move on with her future with Erik.

Sitting under the tree, her heart felt like it had been penetrated by the warmth of the sun too. It was like it had more blood rush through it and became fuller with life. Loren smiled.

Wiping her eyes, she heard a bird sing above her in the branches she had just been admiring. It was a lovely song and she hoped she would remember it for the rest of her life. She wanted to remember the song to remind her of the moment she finally forgave herself.

K A Neemeyer

Chapter 29

After leaving the hospital, Erik, although not very good on crutches, was ready to go home. She cautiously drove to his house to get him some clothes and other items. Leaving Erik to sit in the car, Loren went to the front door and opened it. As the door swung open, she was greeted by a very excited dog. Loren rubbed Sheena's head as she spoke. "Sheena, I just saw you a couple hours ago. Don't you ever get enough attention? Oh well, you're coming home with me now anyways. I'm sure Sam will give you the attention you want."

With Sheena trailing right behind her, Loren went into Erik's bedroom and began to go through his dresser drawers to get a week's worth of undergarments, pajamas, and shorts. She then proceeded to the closet to grab a few shirts and then headed towards the kitchen. There she grabbed Sheena's food and treats.

When Sheena saw her get her food, she began to run in circles and pant hard. Loren laughed at the dog and attached a leash on to her collar. They both headed outside and Loren saw Erik smiling at her from the Jeep. She grinned at him and headed to the back end and opened the door for Sheena to jump in.

On the way home, Loren could hear Sheena panting. When she looked back in the mirror, she could see slobber dripping onto her car seat and down the side. Loren shuddered. She didn't like the idea of having to clean up after a dog and knew it would be like this in the house too.

Finally arriving home, Jessie and Sam came out the front door.

Sam ran to the back of the Jeep to retrieve Sheena. "I finally have a dog. I'm so happy." She looked at Sheena. "I hope you're happy here too. I'll spend so much time with you." Sam hugged Sheena's neck and held her leash as she jumped onto the ground.

Sheena began to pull on the leash as she tried to sniff the ground.

Sam attempted to hold on and was pulled around like a ragdoll as the larger dog became familiar with her new surroundings. She laughed as she ran to keep up and pulled on the leash with all her strength.

Loren watched her daughter and Sheena for a moment as she walked around to the other side of the Jeep. Jessie got there the same time as she did and they smiled as they watched Sheena pull Sam and Sam yell "whoa" like the dog was a horse.

Loren pointed at Sam then began to laugh. "This is going to be interesting. It's definitely going to be an adjustment." She thought of the back seat with slobber on it. "I think I'm going to have to adjust more than anyone else."

Jessie patted her on the back before she opened the front door. "It'll be fine sis. You'll get used to the hair and drool in no time at all."

Erik tried to turn to exit the Jeep and grunted. "She's a good dog. The good in her outweighs the bad stuff. I'm sure she'll mesh well in a couple days' time. Now, help me get out of this thing. I want to stretch my leg out more." He looked at Loren. "It's nice to finally be home."

Loren felt her heart skip a beat. She smiled at him. "Yes it is, isn't it? I have the couch ready for you with a table beside it and the remote close by. And I got the bedroom ready too so that you don't run into anything with your leg. Good thing the master bedroom is on the main floor huh? Otherwise the couch would be your bed for a few days."

Erik smiled. "Well, I imagine there will be days that the couch is my bed. I'm sure you'll get mad at me for something and kick me out of the bedroom. So it's good to try it out to see how comfortable it is."

Loren pushed the hair out of her face, glared at him, and then smiled. "You plan on doing bad stuff already? This *is* going to be an adjustment, isn't it?"

Erik balanced his weight on the crutches and headed towards the front door. "No, I said that you'll get mad at me. Not that I'll necessarily do anything bad. I'm sure there will be something that you misconstrue."

Loren opened the front door and looked back at Erik. "I don't think it's me that misinterprets things. It's been you that does that."

Jessie threw her hands in the air. "I'm glad that I'm moving out. You two would drive me crazy. You already are."

Loren and Erik laughed.

Erik hobbled to the couch and winced when he sat down. "This hurts." He looked at Loren sincerely. "I'm sorry again for scaring you, but I didn't have any control of the situation."

Loren grabbed a pillow to put under his leg. "I already told you that it's fine. It's been four days. I'm over it Erik."

Erik held on to his leg as he lifted it for Loren to put the pillow beneath it. "I know. But I also know how you looked when I first saw you in the hospital. I'm sure old emotions were seeping into your mind." He looked around the room. "Well, at least I finally get to move in. I just didn't think it would take something so drastic to finally get me in here to stay."

Loren hit him on the shoulder with a pillow. "Ha-ha. I only grabbed you enough clothes for a week."

Jessie sat in a chair next to the couch. "I think he's right. I don't know why he hadn't moved in already. Well, that is, before I moved in."

Loren glanced at both of them. "Hey. Don't gang up on me. We just got engaged a little while ago. I don't want Sam getting the wrong impression."

Jessie smirked. "I think she had that when I was living with Derik and not being married. Don't you think?"

"She's my daughter. Not yours. I'm the one that has to instill the right values. I'm trying to do that the best I can."

Jessie stretched and acted like she was bored. "Yeah. Yeah. She's going to form her own opinions too. You've done a good job. Don't think that I don't think that."

Erik groaned. "Hey, how about a little help for the injured man. Don't I come first right now?"

Loren sat next to him and batted her eyes. "I'm sorry your majesty. What can we humble servants do for you?"

Erik got a mischievous smile on his face. "Well, I could think of a lot of things that you could do to make me feel better."

Loren grunted. "Erik. I meant to get you a pillow or something to eat."

Jessie rolled her eyes and stood up. "Yeah. This is getting a little too personal for my taste. I think I'll grab Sam and take some boxes to my apartment."

Loren watched as Jessie headed outside. She still couldn't believe that her sister was moving out and that she had Erik moving in. Leaning on his shoulder, she sighed. "Things sure are changing. And fast. I hope you understand that it's going to take me a bit to get used to all of this." Loren paused for a moment and sat up straight like someone pinched her. "Oh my gosh. You can't look in my closet. My wedding gown is in there."

Erik giggled. "I can't even get to the bathroom without troubles. I don't think I would be wandering into your closet anytime soon. Your gown is safe from my eyes looking at it. Besides that, I want to see you in the dress as you walk down the aisle towards me to be married."

"I want that too."

Just then the front door opened and Loren heard Sam yelling at Sheena to slow down. Then, Sheena came bursting through the door with the leash dragging behind her. She was overly rambunctious as she went bolting through the kitchen and then the living room. Her four feet slid across the wood floor as she tried to turn a corner too fast and she slid into the wall. Not seeming to phase her, Sheena continued to ransack through the rooms, sniffing everything as she went. Finally, when she saw Erik, she jumped onto the couch and sat right on Loren.

Loren shrieked. "Get off me dog. This isn't okay. Get off me."

Sam ran into the house and started laughing. She grabbed Sheena's collar and pulled her off the couch. "That was so funny. You should have seen your face mom."

Loren wasn't amused. "That dog does not get on this sofa, or me. I don't need hair and the smell of dirty dog everywhere."

Kneeling down beside Sheena, Sam pouted. "Are you going to make us get rid of her? She just got here mom. She has to get use to the house just like we have to get use to her."

Loren sighed. "I haven't had a dog since I was younger. Even then, it was a small dog." She looked at Erik and saw him smirking. "It's not funny. Why couldn't you have found a cat on the side of the road? Or a guinea pig?"

Erik started laughing. "Gees Loren. How did you react when you had a new born baby and dirty diapers? Or for that matter, how'd you react when Sam was teething and drooling everywhere or throwing up?"

Standing up, Loren glared back at Erik. "Maybe I'm overreacting a little, but I wasn't ready for all of this. Jessie moving out, you're moving in, and now a dog too. This is a lot to take in." She looked at Sam who was still hugging Sheena's neck. "And no, I'm not going to get rid of her. I'm sure she's a great dog and will be good to have around." Loren looked down at Sheena who was panting heavily and almost looked like she was smiling. "And for you pooch, no drooling everywhere. Okay?" she said not expecting the dog to answer her.

Sam stood up and threw her arms into the air in celebration. "Yay! I have a dog. I'm going to show her my room and see if she'll lay on my bed with me."

Loren watched as Sam and Sheena bounded up the stairs. She smiled and liked to see her little girl so happy. Although, she didn't know how she would get along with a furry friend in the house, but she would put in her best effort.

Just as Loren went to sit back down her phone rang. It was the coffee shop. They were having a problem with one of the machines and needed Loren's help to fix it. Loren groaned and hung up the phone. "Well, I have to head into town and help at the store. Do you want me to have Jessie stay here while I'm gone? Or have Sam stay home?"

Erik looked at his leg and grimaced. "I think I'll be okay, but can you get me some ice to put on my leg before you go." He flashed her a smile. "Maybe a kiss before you go too. It would make me feel a lot better."

Loren shook her head and walked to the kitchen to get an ice pack. When she handed to Erik, he grabbed her hand and pulled her down beside him. Then he put his hand behind her head and gently drew her closer until they were just inches apart.

Loren tried to breathe in his smell of cologne and after shave, but only smelled the hospital. She wrinkled her nose but then kissed Erik softly. She pulled away and looked at him lovingly in the eyes. "Erik? Sweet Erik? When I get back home you need to take a shower. I'll put a bench in there so you can sit down, but you really need a shower. You smell like the hospital does. Not a very attractive smell."

"Well, I was there a few days. I suppose the sweet aroma of the hospital would be attracted to me just like you are," he said jokingly.

Chapter 30

*T*he next couple days were difficult for Loren. Between helping Erik, adjusting to Jessie being gone and not having the extra help, and having a new dog, Loren was drained.

Taking a drink of her dark coffee, Loren tried to gather her thoughts. She looked around her kitchen, scanned the mess, and frowned. She knew after she got home from work that she would have to cook and clean and that made her feel even more exhausted.

Sheena slowly strolled into the room and sat by her side. She stared at Loren with big brown eyes.

Loren patted the dog's head and smiled. "What do you want mutt? I suppose you want a treat to show you were a good dog during the night?"

Sheena panted and wagged her tail.

Loren went to the cabinet to get Sheena a treat. When she handed her the treat, Sam walked into the room and gleamed.

"I knew you'd like her. I just knew you would," Sam said excitedly.

Smiling, Loren sat back down and wrapped her hands around the warm cup of coffee. "Just because I got her a treat doesn't mean I like her. It just means I appreciated that she was quiet last night and didn't wake me up."

Sam sat in a chair next to Loren and sighed. "I want you to like her. It would make it so much better. I mean, she's a good puppy and has slept with me the last couple nights. I've taken her for walks, I've played with her, and I've even brushed her to get some of the extra fur out. I've been doing everything I can to make it easier to have her here. I'm trying mom."

Loren stared at her daughter lovingly. She couldn't believe how grown up she had become over the summer. It scared her that she was going to lose her little girl to a young woman too fast. "Sammie bear. You're a wonderful person. I don't tell you that enough." She directed her attention towards Sheena and watched her lean against Sam's chair. "And I know she's a good dog. I guess I like her a little."

Sam stood up and put her hands in the air in triumph. "Yes! I knew it."

"What do you know?" Erik asked as he hobbled into the kitchen on crutches.

"That mom likes Sheena."

Erik winked at Loren then gave Sam a hug. "Of course she does. Why wouldn't she?" He looked towards the sink and sighed. "I think I'll try to do some dishes today. I need to try and pull my weight around here more, even if I am on crutches."

Loren stood up and gave him a hug. "You don't have to. I'll get it done after work." She looked at her watch. "I'd better get my butt in gear or the boss might fire me."

Sam rolled her eyes. "That's getting old. You've used that line a million times. It was funny when I was like, seven."

Shaking her head, Loren headed towards her bedroom to finish getting dressed. When she was putting her hair back in a ponytail, she heard Jessie's voice holler from the living room. Loren rushed out to see her and Cody standing together.

Cody had his arm around Jessie's waist and looked happy. "Good morning Loren. We thought we'd get a few more boxes. Or I should say, she's forcing me to help her get a few more boxes."

Jessie softly elbowed Cody in the ribs. "That's not nice. You said you'd love to help me." She gave him a kiss on the cheek and grinned. "And I said I'd make it worth your while."

Cody blushed and looked down at the wood floor. "Hey, there's a child in the room."

Sam got a confused look. "I don't get it."

Everyone laughed.

Loren watched as they all conversed. Sam sat on the couch with Sheena close to her side, Cody and Jessie hugged each other and looked content, and Erik looked comfortable to be there. Loren never thought she could feel so much love in one place. She had the most important people in her life, right in front of her, and she felt wonderful. She fidgeted with the ring on her finger and knew it was all going to work out. She looked down at her watch again and frowned. "Well, I have to get going. I hope you all have a good day and I'll see you tonight."

Erik gave her a hug and kissed her passionately. "I hope you think of me because I'll be thinking of you. I love you Loren."

Loren headed towards the door and looked back one more time. She couldn't help but to smile as she closed the door behind her and headed to "Good Mornings".

When she arrived to work, it was busy. Time seemed to fly by with each customer and purchase. Loren barely had a chance to sit down between stocking shelves and getting coffee for people. When she finally had a minute to herself, she headed to her office and shut the door. She leaned back in her chair, played with the necklace around her neck, and thought of Craig.

She wondered if he watched over them. She wondered if he saw how successful their shop had become and smiled down at her for the accomplishment. She wondered if he was happy for her choices and thought she was doing a good job with Sam.

Her thoughts were interrupted by a knock on the door. It was Amber saying that they had a swarm of customers again and needed her help. Loren stretched her shoulders and headed out the door. And after what seemed to be a couple hours, instead of eight, Loren locked the doors and headed home.

As she came to the intersection to head to her house, her thoughts went back to Craig. She suddenly wanted to talk to him and needed to talk to him. So, instead of turning right, she turned left and headed to his burial plot.

Knowing right where to go, Loren weaved through the gravestones. She walked past the monument of an angel blowing a trumpet, past the water fountain with the small angel holding a vase, and past the tall Linden tree. When she saw the stone with the black polished double heart tombstone, she knew she was at her destination.

Loren ran her hand along the polished stone. She read the inscription on the heart to the left side and felt her heart break like it did every time she read it. Then she glanced at the heart with only her name and began to cry.

She sat down on the ground and hugged her legs. She cried until there were no more tears then looked up at the tombstone again. "I miss you Craig. I miss you with all my heart and soul. There are times that I'm so mad at you for leaving me." Loren exhaled loudly. "Why did you have to leave me? We were meant to be together forever, at least I thought we were. I miss you Craig."

Loren let her thoughts float away. She imagined Sam so ecstatic to have Sheena and Jessie wrapped in Cody's arms so happy together. She could see the sparkle in Erik's eyes when he looked at her and that made her feel loved. Loren knew she was blissfully in love with Erik.

Hearing the tree's leaves begin to rustle with the breeze and the fountain in the distance, Loren thought back to her time at the hospital. She remembered feeling free and satisfied with her decisions.

She looked back towards the stone and traced the letters of Craig's name. "I'm happy again. I know I told you about Erik before, but I finally realized how much I love him. I love him so much, but I need you to understand that I'll always have a place in my heart for you. It will never be extinguished. It couldn't be. What you and I had was something wonderful and magical, but Erik and I have something special too." She thought of Sam. "He treats Sammie bear really good. He has never raised his voice to her and tries all he can to make her happy. He tries all he can to make me happy."

Loren listened to the leaves moving and felt the breeze in her hair. She looked up at the tall tree and watched as the leaves moved like dancers so elegantly. Still looking at the tree, she continued to talk. "I hope you're happy that I'm happy. I hope you're sitting up on a cloud watching us and wanting us to move on because I have to move on. I have to continue this journey of life and try to get the most love out of it as I can. And I think I would be most successful with Erik by my side. He is a wonderful man." She looked back towards Craig's name and smiled. "I know you would be. You always told me that I have a big heart and need to express the love I have in it. You always told me that you wanted me to be forever happy and I believe you."

Loren clutched the necklace around her neck. She knew what she had to do.

Slowly, Loren removed the necklace and wrapped the chain around her hand. She grinned as she watched the light reflect off the diamonds within the gold heart. She spoke softly. "When you gave me this necklace, I thought it was the most beautiful piece of jewelry, and I still do. It has become so much more than a plain necklace. It has become a symbol of our life together. I feel like it represents everything we had. The love we felt for one another and our devotion to each other." Loren unwrapped the necklace from her hand and let it dangle in the air. "I will never forget what we had, but I have to move on."

Shaking her head, Loren sat up on her knees, grabbed a stick, and dug a shallow hole. Then, very gently, she laid the necklace within the hole and covered it with fresh dirt. Patting it down softly, she stood up and looked back at the tombstone. "Thank you for the time we had together. You made me a better person and you gave me Samantha. I can see you through her smile and know you'll always be with her. I know you want my heart to be free so that I can love Erik the best I can. I will always love you."

Walking away, Loren felt free to love with her whole heart again. She could finally allow herself to love Erik like he deserved. The guilt she had created not wanting to betray her and Craig's love was gone. She smiled and somehow knew that burying the necklace had just released the chains from her heart.

Made in the USA
San Bernardino, CA
13 October 2014